A FRESH START ON CRUMCAREY

CRUMCAREY ISLAND - BOOK 5

BETH RAIN

Copyright © 2024 by Beth Rain

A Fresh Start on Crumcarey (Crumcarey Island: Book 5)

First Publication: 4th October, 2024

All rights reserved.

No part of this book may be reproduced in any form or by any electronic or mechanical means, including information storage and retrieval systems. Except for use in any review, the reproduction or utilization of this work, in whole or in part, in any form by any electronic, mechanical or other means now known or hereafter invented, is forbidden without the written permission of the publisher.

Published by Beth Rain. The author may be contacted by email on bethrainauthor@gmail.com

 Created with Vellum

CHAPTER 1

MAGGIE

'Just one more bite,' Maggie wheedled, as though she was trying to convince a toddler to eat her breakfast.

It wasn't a stroppy two-year-old she was having to persuade to scoff the slightly stale piece of toast, though – it was herself. Thirty-three years old, but admittedly still a little bit stroppy... and *more* than a bit nervous.

'Nope,' she muttered, shaking her head and tossing the barely touched toast back onto her chipped plate. There was no way she could force down any more of it... not with the mad whirl of butterflies going on in her stomach.

Straightening up from her slump at the rickety kitchen table that was little more than a piece of manky hardboard balancing on a couple of cardboard boxes, Maggie forced herself to take a deep breath. 'Finish your drink at any rate!'

Grabbing the rainbow mug, she took a mouthful of gritty coffee and grimaced. *Gross!*

'At least I'll be able to get a decent coffee when I get to work!'

Work.

The squirming in Maggie's stomach stepped up a notch, and she let out a groan. Today, she was going to be re-joining the world after playing hermit for well over a year... and she didn't think she'd ever felt this nervous in her entire life.

Maggie glanced at her watch. She had about ten minutes before she had to leave for her first-ever shift at The Tallyaff – and she had to admit, she was dreading it.

'Come on Mags, you're being ridiculous,' she sighed, rubbing her stomach and wishing it would calm down a bit. From what she knew of Olive Martinelli – owner of The Tallyaff and person in charge of pretty much everything that happened on the island – the woman was a sweetheart. She was bound to make an awesome boss too.

It wasn't the job itself that was worrying her either. Maggie wasn't afraid of hard work, and she'd done plenty of customer-facing jobs to see her through college – so this wasn't her first rodeo. The work should be simple enough to wrap her head around. She was going to be helping Olive with everything from making up the guest bedrooms to serving behind the bar and restocking the little shop. There would be lots to learn, but she was sure she'd be able to pick things up fast enough.

No... the reason her stomach felt like it was trying to escape through her mouth was far less rational than that. What if she'd forgotten how to talk to other people while she'd been hiding away in the cottage? After all, it had been over a year since Russell had pulled his disappearing act. Since then, most of Maggie's in-depth conversations had been with herself.

'You'll be fine, dumbass!' she muttered forcing a smile onto her face – just for the practice. It felt... strange. Surely this whole "how to be human" thing would come back to her pretty quickly... wouldn't it? After all, she'd had a tight group of friends down south before she'd relocated. Back then, she'd had no problem chatting away, making small talk... being "normal."

A lot had happened since then, though.

Maggie took another deep breath. The last thing she needed today was to turn up at work doing a good impression of a gibbering wreck!

Maybe if she focussed on the positives, it would help...

For one thing, Olive wouldn't have given her the job if she didn't think she was up to it. For another, Maggie was good with faces. She knew most of the locals... though maybe not *quite* as well as she should, considering she'd lived on Crumcarey for more than a year and a half. Still, at least she'd be able to tell them apart from the ever-increasing number of tourists who were flocking to stay on the island!

Actually, that counted as another good thing, didn't it? The recently released updated island guidebook had been a huge hit. Combined with the new runway at the airport, the replacement ferry that had taken over while the old boat was being re-fitted, and the wave of interest surrounding the standing stones near the castle, it felt like Crumcarey was on the up-and-up. The Tallyaff was busier than ever… which was the reason Olive had a job to offer her in the first place.

Yes, there were plenty of positives to be grateful for… so why was her idiot heart still trying to beat its way out of her ribcage?

Maggie swallowed. The answer to that was easy enough. The Tallyaff was at the heart of the community – a community she'd done very little to become a part of since moving to the island.

It wouldn't be too bad though… would it? Hopefully, the locals would get used to having her around soon enough. It would be fine… and even if it wasn't, she had to man-up anyway. She needed this job… and not just because of the very necessary cash injection.

At long last, Maggie had come to the realisation that if she wanted to stay in her cottage and make the place at least vaguely inhabitable before winter descended, she needed help. To get that help, she needed to break her self-imposed isolation. As much as she would love to be able to renovate her home single-handedly, it just wasn't possible. Which meant it was time to crawl out from beneath her stone and find her place in the community at long last.

When Maggie had first arrived on the island with Russell, he'd been adamant that it would be better to keep themselves to themselves. Back then, she'd been happy enough to go along with it. After all, they'd been in the honeymoon period of their adventure – a new life together on a remote island doing up a tumbledown cottage and turning it into their dream home. There had been something quite romantic about the whole thing. It had been the pair of them against the world. Or… that's what she'd thought, at least.

The move had been Russell's idea – and he'd sold the dream of it to her hook, line and sinker. He'd convinced her to sell her flat and put all the money towards their new home on Crumcarey. They'd bought the little cottage without even visiting to view it first. On the journey north, they'd made each other a promise that they wouldn't ask for any help. Whatever work was needed, they'd get stuck in and learn how to do it all themselves. Together.

'Look how well that turned out!' muttered Maggie, getting to her feet and shoving her chair backwards. The legs promptly caught on an uneven flagstone and it tipped over with a clatter.

Doing her best to hold in a growl, Maggie grabbed the chair and set it back on its feet. Thinking about Russell and all his broken promises always turned her into a bear with a sore head. She might be over him—just about, anyway—but she wasn't over the sense of betrayal yet. In fact, she wasn't sure she'd ever get over that part.

All Russell's promises of tackling this adventure together had disappeared the minute he'd been offered a job back on the mainland. A huge salary, first-class travel, and an obscene expenses account - that's all it had taken for him to leave her behind. They'd barely been on Crumcarey six months when he'd disappeared off to make the most of "the opportunity of a lifetime". The irony hadn't been lost on Maggie – they were the exact same words he'd used when he'd been busy talking her into buying this very cottage.

And then… he was just gone.

Russell hadn't even bothered to officially split up with her – he'd just upped and left. Postcards still arrived now and then from the exotic locations his new job took him to… but he never came back, not even to visit.

Maggie didn't really understand the point of the cards. Perhaps they made him feel better about abandoning her at the edge of the world in a house with very little roof. Or maybe he really *did* mean to come back one day. She shuddered. He was most definitely *not* welcome.

Of course, Maggie knew she could have sold up and moved back down south. It would have probably been the sensible thing to do. In fact, the minute she'd admitted to her friends what had happened, they'd practically demanded she got on with it pronto. If she'd been any closer, she had a feeling they might have turned up en mass and physically dragged her back to her old stomping grounds.

As much as she was grateful for their staunch support from a distance - Maggie was glad they hadn't. She'd already fallen in love with the island and its big skies, lolling seals and cheeky puffins. She even loved its mad weather – when it wasn't ripping the tarpaulins off the roof. Maggie wasn't sure of much – but she did know that she didn't want to live anywhere else.

That said… she didn't want to live like this anymore, either.

Letting out a long sigh, Maggie checked her watch again.

'Shoes. Shoes would be good right now,' she muttered, mooching through the cottage and doing her best not to look too closely at her surroundings as she went. Her dream home was fast deteriorating into a nightmare, and she could do without the sight of it causing any more flutterings of anxiety right now.

It had been a long time since she'd looked at her early drawings of the place – outlining a cute, cosy cottage full of light and charm. She'd shut her grand plans in a plastic box long before Russell had left, and by this point, Maggie could barely remember the sense of hope she'd felt when she'd sketched them.

Now, her sad cottage was little more than a ruin. It was at least eighty per cent tarpaulin, and the remaining twenty per cent was made up of expanding spray foam and bits of hardboard tacked to the walls in an attempt to stop the outside from feeling quite so... *inside.*

Every time she made a grocery run, Maggie grabbed another can or two of foam. It didn't help much, and she was under no illusions... the cottage was slowly crumbling around her ears. One thing was for sure, there was no way it would make it through another winter in one piece. Not without help.

Clambering across her mattress that lay directly in front of the door to her bedroom – the only spot where she could guarantee she wouldn't get dripped on while she slept - Maggie started hunting around for a semi-decent pair of shoes that weren't covered in paint, silicon sealant or expanding foam.

Olive had told her not to worry too much about what to wear to work – but Maggie wanted to look at least halfway presentable. Even that was going to be a challenge considering she lived in a cross between a barn and a construction site! She'd already had to pull on a ridiculous pair of black skinny jeans that hadn't seen the light of day since she'd moved to the island... but clean shoes were going to be even trickier to find.

Sure enough, the only pairs hiding in the corner of

her bedroom with the spiders were her wellies and her safety boots—and there was no way she was going to turn up to work wearing either! They were both grubby, grotty and splattered in paint.

Maggie was sure she had a pair of lightweight black pumps around somewhere. They were so unbelievably impractical against Crumcarey's less-than-clement weather conditions that she hadn't worn them since the move… which meant there was a slim chance they might still be vaguely presentable.

'What did I do with them?' she muttered, heaving herself back to her feet and swiping at the dust on her knees. Maybe she'd binned them. She certainly hadn't seen them for a long time…

'Ah ha!'

Dashing through to the bathroom, Maggie grabbed the giant plastic clip-lock tub where she stashed her towels, washcloths and bedding to keep them from getting damp. Hoisting it out of the way, she uncovered a second, identical tub underneath. It was full to the brim with random bits and bobs she'd wanted to save from the less-than-loving attention of the leaky roof.

'Bingo!' she cheered, popping off the lid and dragging the pair of pumps out from beneath an ancient teddy bear onesie. They were mercifully clear of paint splatters, and even better – they were dry.

'Hmm… speaking of dry…'

Grabbing a stack of buckets from beside the sink, Maggie eyeballed the exposed underside of the roof slates, hunting for the tell-tale patch of sky visible through the cracks. As soon as she spotted the sliver of grumpy-looking clouds overhead, she popped one of the buckets directly beneath it. There was a good chance it might rain while she was at work, and she didn't fancy the idea of having to grab a mop the minute she got home.

Heading back through to the open plan kitchen and living room, Maggie quickly deployed the rest of the buckets in the usual spots - just in case. She had tarpaulins covering the worst of the leaks, but the way the rain came down some days, they simply didn't stand a chance. Besides, a couple of the tarps needed replacing - again. It was yet another job she needed to add to her ever-expanding list that resembled more of a scroll by this point. In fact, she needed to remember to ask Olive if she'd order some more for her.

'Tarpaulin Girl strikes again,' she sighed, flopping down onto the beaten-up old sofa to pull on her pumps. She knew that was the locals' pet name for her…

Maggie breathed out a slow sigh of relief as the butterflies finally eased up a bit. It was possibly the weirdest thing in the world to offer any kind of comfort… but surely the fact that she'd been given a nickname must mean she'd been accepted by the locals… at least a little bit?

Maggie shrugged. Either way, there were definitely worst things to be called.

CHAPTER 2

LUKE

Rolling his shoulders, Luke threw down the oily rag he'd been using to wipe his hands and yawned. He needed a break. He'd been on the go since the sun came up… and he wasn't planning on stopping until it got dark. Not while there were people to help and jobs to do… and there were *always* plenty of jobs to keep him busy when he visited Crumcarey!

Still, a scalding-hot cup of coffee and a pastry or two were definitely in order right now. Luckily, working on Olive's two hire cars out in the car park of The Tallyaff meant the tasty treats were in *very* easy reach.

Gently closing the bonnet of the car lovingly called the *Cow Taxi* by the locals – on account of the rather pungent scent that clung to its interior – Luke yawned again. He hadn't stopped since he'd arrived on the island a little over three weeks ago. Not that he minded, of course. Luke liked to be busy.

First, he'd focused on helping Connor with the refit of the ferry during the day, while his evenings were taken up with settling into one of the barns up at the farm. The farmhouse was plenty big enough for him of course, but night times there were filled with terrifying grunts, groans and growls that drifted from his uncle's bedroom. McGregor, his uncle's scruffy little terrier, got all the blame, but Luke was pretty sure they were both involved.

Either way, Luke had commandeered one of the less decrepit outbuildings. It had a decent roof and power, and that was really all he needed. He'd worked to make himself as comfortable as possible and had managed to get hot and cold water installed as well as an old wood burner his uncle had been using to prop up one end of a workbench.

It was cosy, comfortable, and just what Luke needed - though perhaps he'd done too good a job on the place considering Uncle Harris kept threatening to move in with him!

He hadn't quite managed to finish it off yet, though. Ray Young over at Crum House had asked him to take a look at the heating for the swimming pool, and there was no way Luke could say no to that considering his uncle was probably the pool's most regular visitor. After that was fixed, he'd moved on to helping Ray with some modifications on the boat for the new dive school.

Now here he was, tinkering away with Olive's hire car fleet. He wasn't entirely sure two stinky old cars really warranted the word "fleet", but Olive was adamant that it looked better on the island's website.

'Well, that's you sorted, old thing!' he muttered, giving the Cow Taxi a pat. Apparently, it had been stuck in second gear for months. Well – not anymore! Next, he needed to have a look underneath the other car – the aptly named Chicken Bus. He wanted to see if he could attach something to the bottom of the exhaust pipe to stop it clanking as it trundled around Crumcarey's bumpy roads.

But first… coffee!

As he ambled towards the door of The Tallyaff, Luke made a mental note that he actually needed to spend some time with Uncle Harris while he was on the island. He'd been so busy since he'd arrived that the pair of them had been a bit like ships passing in the night. They'd always got on like a house on fire - sharing the naughty corner during the rare Harris family get-togethers, and spending time with him was a joy.

Not that Mr Harris was *really* Luke's uncle in the strictest sense of the word. He was pretty sure there should be a "great" or two in there somewhere. The old man had always argued that the word *great* made him feel ancient though – so he'd adopted *Uncle Harris* as his official title – and that's the way it had been ever since Luke had spent his school holidays on the farm as a young lad.

Luke had to admit that he was glad he hadn't left this visit too much longer – the old place was looking decidedly worse for wear compared to the last time he'd stayed. Crumcarey's weather was notoriously rough on houses and outbuildings – especially when routine maintenance wasn't kept up with. His uncle's age, combined with an ankle injury that had taken forever to improve, seemed to have contributed to his slowdown.

'Slowdown my foot!' chuckled Luke, letting himself into the little porch of the guesthouse and pausing to toe off his muddy boots.

The only concession his uncle seemed to have given his bad leg was to accept regular swimming sessions with Anna up at Crum House to work on strengthening it. Other than that, he'd been full of his usual madcap plans.

From what Ray had been telling him, they'd come very close to having a petting zoo on the island. But Uncle Harris preferred talking about his plans to putting them into action. In fact, it was one of his favourite topics of conversation – coming second only to complaining about the tourists clogging up the island's roads.

'Right… time for a sit-down,' said Luke, preparing himself for Olive Martinelli's bouncy brand of small talk. With one last yawn for good measure, he pushed his way into the gleaming golden bar room of The Tallyaff.

'Good morning Luke! You look like you could do with a coffee… and maybe a pastry or two?'

Luke snapped his mouth shut mid-yawn and stared at the woman behind the bar. That was definitely *not* Olive Martinelli! In fact… he didn't know who she was. She seemed to know him well enough, though!

'Hi!' he said, desperately trying to place her… while doing his best not to stare. A long dark rope of hair lay over one shoulder and she had him pinned with a pair of soft, caramel eyes.

'Hi!' he said again, clearing his throat and feeling more than a little bit stupid.

He didn't know this person… he was sure of it. He would have *definitely* remembered meeting her… considering that the look she was giving him was making his knees turn to jelly.

It was strange – he thought he knew everyone on Crumcarey. After all, the island wasn't exactly large. Of course, there was no keeping up with the steady stream of visitors… but this woman clearly wasn't a tourist. For one thing, she was standing behind the bar wearing one of Olive's aprons.

'Hi!' she laughed, shaking her hair out of the way as her eyes danced with humour. 'Your uncle's not in yet… but I'm guessing he'll be here soon.'

'Uh huh?' said Luke, willing his brain to kick into

gear. He might not know *her*, but she definitely knew who he was.

'Why don't you go clean up a bit while I make your cappuccino? Triple shot, no sugar, extra chocolate - right?'

'Erm… right?' said Luke, now feeling totally lost. 'I'll just… bathroom!' he muttered, glancing down at his hands and wrinkling his nose.

Yuck!

There was no telling what might be hiding under his fingernails after tending to the Chicken Bus and the Cow Taxi! Luke scurried away from the bar feeling decidedly discombobulated.

Shoving his way into the bathroom without touching anything with his hands, he turned on the tap… and smiled as the steaming water distracted him for a moment. It had been one of the first jobs he'd done when he'd arrived. He'd barely stepped off the replacement ferry when Olive had roped him in for a little light maintenance.

Luke didn't mind one bit, of course. He adored Olive and loved the fact that he could lend a hand whenever he reappeared on the island. It hadn't taken long to get the hot water flowing again. He'd also fixed a couple of dripping taps in the guest rooms while he'd been at it. Of course, he'd arrived without his tools, so Olive had told him to grab anything he needed from the little shop and then just pop them back when he was done.

Luke took his time to dry his hands, buying himself a few moments to get his head together before heading back out into the bar. He wanted to find out about the mystery woman with the dancing eyes… but he'd prefer not to make a total prat out of himself while he was at it.

'What's your problem?' he muttered, eyeballing his reflection in the mirror over the sinks. He never usually had any problems nattering away.

Taking a deep breath, he quickly inspected his face for any flecks of grossness from beneath the bonnets of Olive's hire cars… but it looked like he was in the clear. His overalls were covered with who-knew-what still, but it would look a bit odd if he climbed out of them, wouldn't it?!

'Get a grip!' he tutted, turning and heading straight back out into the bar before he could think himself into a hole.

'Your coffee…' said the woman, gesturing at a steaming cup.

Luke raised his eyebrows as he sat down. Next to the cup was a plate bearing two pastries. There wasn't any butter – just a small pot of tawny marmalade and a knife instead of a spoon.

It was perfect. Breakfast just the way he would have ordered it… except…

'Double espresso?' queried Luke.

'For your uncle,' said the woman.

'But he's not—' he started.

'Behind you!' she said with a grin.

Luke peered over his shoulder just as a scruffy little dog came scurrying into the room – all wagging tail and wiry hair and twitching whiskers.

'You old scruffbag!' said Luke, leaning down to give the little dog's ears a ruffle.

'That's not a very nice way to greet your Uncle!' puffed Mr Harris, bringing up the rear.

Luke grinned at the old man. 'Well… if the shoe fits…!'

'Cheeky so-and-so!' huffed Mr Harris, sinking onto the stool next to him and picking up the espresso seamlessly, as though he'd ordered it in advance. 'Thanks Maggie, just what I need!'

Huh, so his Uncle clearly knew the mysterious Maggie. Excellent – that meant he'd be able to get all the info from him without having to make an idiot out of himself in front of her.

'You look done in!' said Luke, grabbing the marmalade and smothering his first croissant with the entire contents of the tiny pot.

'It's these blasted tourists!' huffed Mr Harris. 'Who'd have thought we'd have rush hour traffic on Crumcarey?!'

'Really?' said Luke with a grin. 'You got stuck in a traffic jam?'

'Two of those idiotic campers in a row, nonetheless,' said Mr Harris, bristling. 'Just a shame I didn't put my foot down and get that petting zoo off the ground. I'd be raking it in by now!'

Luke glanced at Maggie just as she popped a fresh pot of marmalade in front of him. She smiled at him again, her eyes dancing with humour, and Luke felt the bottom fall out of his world.

Who was this woman?!

CHAPTER 3

MAGGIE

Maggie had to admit, she was having a brilliant first morning with Olive. Not only was her new boss kind, but she also had a wicked sense of humour.

To that end, she'd taken Maggie over to a window and pointed out Luke as he was working on the hire cars. Then she'd filled Maggie in on his regular order, the way he preferred everything, and the fact that he was bound to need an extra pot of marmalade. He also always needed to be prompted to wash his hands.

'It'll scare the willies out of him!' chuckled Olive.

Maggie was game. Anything to hear her new boss's infectious laugh. Besides, she was more than happy to have an excuse to talk to the handsome stranger when he finally appeared in the bar.

Luke clearly had no idea who she was, and Maggie was having a grand old time winding him up. If the slightly freaked-out expression on his face was anything to go by, he'd clearly come to the conclusion that she was some kind of witch.

Of course, they might not have met in person before, but Maggie knew exactly who Luke was. Her house wasn't that far from Mr Harris's farm, and she shopped in The Tallyaff often enough to have picked up on the grapevine that Mr Harris was expecting a house guest.

As she dried and stacked clean coffee cups on the ledge above the machine, Maggie took the opportunity to shoot regular glances at the newcomer as he chatted away with his uncle. He was wearing overalls covered in oil and goodness only knew what else… but even so, he was a striking bloke. Short, dark hair, tanned skin that seemed to glisten with health… and those eyes. They were like two ice chips. Bright and almost unnaturally blue. They could have made him look slightly foreboding if it wasn't for the fine fan of wrinkles at the corners – hinting that his gorgeous smile was a regular feature.

Maggie swallowed as her eyes dropped to his large hands wrapped around his almost-empty coffee cup. If ever there was a pair of hands that looked like they knew what they were doing, she was looking at them.

Clearing her throat and averting her eyes as a wave of heat crept up her body, Maggie fumbled with the cup she was drying – only just catching it before it tumbled to the floor.

Oops!

'Steady on, there, Mags!' said Mr Harris, raising a concerned eyebrow in her direction at the sound of rattling china.

'Sorry!' she squeaked.

Mr Harris gave her a long look, and she squirmed. She knew she was being ridiculous – logically, there was no way the old man could know that she'd just been fantasising about his nephew's hands doing all sorts of things… but still…

'Let me get you both a refill,' she muttered. Any excuse to turn her back on the pair of them for a moment.

As she began re-loading the pucks with fresh coffee, Maggie couldn't help but compare Luke to Russell. From what Olive had told her, Luke could fix practically anything he turned his hands to… and had a habit of doing so without even being asked. Russell, on the other hand, had been the polar opposite. Her ex had an overblown opinion of his own abilities – and yet, somehow, he destroyed everything he touched. He used the wrong tools, got the wrong end of the stick, and eventually, anything he "worked on" had to be fixed by someone else… or was just left to leak, squeak, and disintegrate.

The man didn't know his expanding foam from his elbow! Had she really thought that he'd change? That he'd learn and get better with practice? The cottage was in a worse state now than when they'd first moved in – and a good part of that was down to the awful bodge-jobs he'd done around the place.

Maggie set the coffee machine whistling, echoing her mounting frustration as memories of her ex flooded in. She knew she was fast heading down the same old spiral of despair – the one that had kept her out of sight of the rest of the island for months.

The problem was - she felt like an idiot.

For moving to Crumcarey with someone so flaky to start with.

For convincing herself that everything would work out for the best.

For re-convincing herself that she could hack it on her own when he left.

'Earth to Maggie?'

'Huh?' said Maggie, turning to find Olive watching her with one eyebrow raised and a pile of post clutched in her hands.

'You okay?' said Olive warily. 'You look like you're gearing up to murder the coffee machine… though what it's done to you, I have no idea!'

Maggie grimaced. 'Sorry, I was miles away there for a second.'

'Hm,' said Olive. 'Somewhere with palm trees?'

'I… what's that now?' laughed Maggie, shaking her head and doing her best to get rid of the spectre of Russell that was now hanging over her.

'Just wondering if you were somewhere nice,' said Olive. 'Maybe somewhere like this?' She held up a postcard showing a deckchair underneath a palm tree on a golden, sandy beach. In the background, there was a grand-looking hotel with a vast swimming pool.

Maggie felt herself slide even further down her spiral of doom.

A postcard from Russell. Classic timing!

'Okay... now you look like you want to murder your pile of post too!' said Olive, taking a tiny step back as Maggie reached out and took the little bundle from her.

'Just the card,' she muttered.

'Oh...' said Olive. 'Is it from...' she trailed off.

'Russell,' said Maggie with a nod, flipping it over to confirm. Sure enough, there was his familiar, untidy scrawl, along with a stamp that told her he was busy living it up in Dubai.

'I'm sorry,' said Olive. 'I should have hidden it under the other envelopes.'

'It's not your fault my ex is an idiot,' said Maggie as she scanned his brief note. It was the usual drivel.

Having a wonderful time. Wish you were here. See you soon. R x

'Yeah, right,' she muttered, noting the single kiss. They'd definitely decreased in number. As for seeing him soon...

Tearing the card cleanly in half, Maggie shoved it into the pocket of her apron and turned her attention back to the coffees she was making. She promptly decided she'd better start again. They'd been sitting there for far too long and were probably going cold.

'You sure you're okay?' said Olive lightly.

'I'm grand, thanks,' she said, forcing a smile. Because it was true… it had all been going so well… or at least, it had been until the blasted palm trees turned up. 'Hey, Olive? Do you reckon you can put any future postcards from him straight in the bin for me?'

'You've got it!' said Olive, patting her on the shoulder.

CHAPTER 4

LUKE

'I'm telling you, I'd be raking it in with all these visitors!'

Luke grinned and nodded along. He knew it was best just to agree with his uncle when he was on one of his rants.

'I've never seen this road so busy,' continued Mr Harris with a tut. 'It was never like this back in my day. These visitors are a menace!'

Luke raised an eyebrow as he hit the brakes of his uncle's old truck. He didn't say anything, but right now, he had to agree… at least when it came to the visitors just ahead of them. They'd been filling in the paperwork for the Cow Taxi just as he and his uncle had left The Tallyaff. Thirty seconds into their trip home, the ancient hire car had appeared behind them – practically climbing into the back of the truck before overtaking them on the dodgiest of blind bends.

Now they were busy weaving across the road ahead of them, slamming the brakes on every so often so that the passenger could hang out of the window to take photos. Then they'd zoom off again – completely oblivious to the fact that there was another vehicle on the road behind them.

'You do know the roads would be even worse if you *had* opened a petting zoo, don't you?' said Luke lightly.

'Aye,' said Mr Harris, cocking his head. 'That'd be Ray and Anna's problem though, wouldn't it? I was planning to have it up at Crum House, so they'd have to deal with all the extra traffic!'

Luke huffed out a laugh. 'Lucky for them they're too busy then, eh? Sounds like Ray's getting on well with the dive school!'

'Aye,' said his uncle again. 'Though he's half the problem – encouraging all these visitors.'

'I know you don't really mean that,' Luke grinned.

'Do too,' muttered Mr Harris, ruffling the ears of the sleeping dog in his lap. 'You know, McGregor hates the tourists too. He's exhausted. Lots more barking to be done with all these extra people around. I've never known the poor lad to sleep so much!'

Luke grunted at that. He didn't want to be the one to point out that the feisty little terrier was simply getting on a bit.

'More visitors means more money on the island,' said Luke. 'And it means the places you love – places like The Tallyaff - will not just survive but thrive.'

'True,' said Mr Harris. 'Olive's thriving alright. She's booked solid for weeks. All the rooms are full, and the shop's busier than ever too – that's why she's had to go and bring in the new girl!'

Luke gripped the steering wheel tightly. He'd been hoping to swing the conversation around to the mysterious Maggie at some point – preferably in a way that wouldn't alert Uncle Harris to the fact that he had anything other than a passing curiosity in the beautiful new barmaid. Unfortunately – if the look his uncle was now giving him was anything to go by – Mr Harris had already clocked that he'd spent a bit too much time staring at the way her dark hair came alive with thousands of tiny golden lights under the lamps of The Tallyaff.

'Bonnie lass, mind...' said his uncle with a decidedly roguish grin.

'I hadn't noticed,' said Luke flatly, slamming on his brakes again. The Cow Taxi had just swerved across the road ahead of them to give the photographer a better angle of a crumbling cottage.

'Hadn't noticed, eh?' chuckled Mr Harris. 'Be off with you lad, your eyes were out on stalks!'

Alarm bells started ringing somewhere inside Luke's head, and he glanced at his Uncle. 'They weren't... were they? I mean... she wouldn't have noticed... I mean, she wouldn't have thought that...'

'Calm down, lad!' said Mr Harris kindly. 'It's just

that I know you well enough to see the signs. You might get a bit of a ribbing from Olive, mind!'

'I can handle Olive,' said Luke tightly. 'But… you don't think Maggie—'

'Your Maggie won't have noticed a thing,' said Mr Harris calmly. 'I'd say she had enough on her mind to keep her distracted.'

'She's *not* my Maggie,' said Luke. 'I've never met her before… though she seems to know who I am…'

'Course she does,' said Mr Harris with a shrug. 'She's a local, and we locals know everything.'

'I guessed she must be – working at the Tallyaff and all,' said Luke. 'But… I don't even know where she lives.'

'Right there,' said Mr Harris, pointing at the sad, broken-down little cottage just ahead of them.

'You're not serious?' gasped Luke, watching as the tourists swerved in a great arc before speeding away from the cottage after taking their fill of photos. 'Someone *lives* in that?!'

Luke had barely even glanced at the place before. It was a complete wreck – little more than a ruin. He couldn't remember anyone living there in all the years he'd been coming to Crumcarey.

'I'm dead serious,' said Mr Harris, nodding. 'Take a look for yourself if you don't believe me.'

Luke put the truck back in gear and crawled forward so that he could take a closer look. The cottage looked even worse up close. There were tattered tarpaulins strung together everywhere – mostly across different parts of the roof, though it was clear that Crumcarey's ever-present wind had been playing havoc with them.

Here and there, he could see the tell-tale spots of what looked like bright orange fungus mushrooming from the walls. It was clear someone had been busy with a can or ten of expanding foam – doing their best to fill in some of the gaps. Where the holes were too large for the foam to be of any help, square fenceposts the locals called "stabs" were wedged into the ground – their pointy, tapered ends holding sheets of hardboard in place against the walls.

One or two of the windows were missing panes of glass. In the gaps, he could see bits of cardboard, plastic and tin. One of the frames was being held in place with a piece of wood so flimsy, it looked like it might give way at any moment.

'I'm guessing she's only just moved in?' said Luke.

'Then you're guessing wrong,' said Mr Harris. 'Our Maggie's been in there coming up to two years.'

'In *that* mess?!' gasped Luke.

'Aye,' said Mr Harris. 'And we're all pretty impressed with her staying power, I can tell you.'

'Is she… erm…' Luke paused. He wanted to know if she was on her own in the crumbling cottage, but he knew if he asked that particular question, his uncle would be on it like a dog with a bone.

'Tarpaulin Girl – that's what we call her,' chuckled

Mr Harris fondly, seemingly unaware of Luke's conundrum. 'She's one of those special people who arrives on the island – and stays.'

'What a name!' laughed Luke. 'She sounds like some kind of superhero.'

'Living like that?' said Mr Harris. 'I'd say she is. Even superheroes need a hand sometimes, though. We all want to help her out… but we don't want to intrude. You know how it is. She's got to make the first move. Maybe now she's working for Olive, we'll all get the chance to know her a bit better… and then we'll see what we can do.'

'Well… she's definitely brave,' said Luke seriously. 'I'm not sure I'd be up for staying a single night in that place!'

'Strange what people will do for love, isn't it?' said Mr Harris thoughtfully.

Luke felt a lead weight settle in his stomach. Love? So there was a *Mr* Tarpaulin Girl, then? He didn't know why that should bother him so much… maybe because there was no way he'd have put up with *his* Maggie living in that state for so long.

If she was his.

Which she wasn't.

Of course.

'Love?' said Luke, wanting his uncle to go on, but not really sure what else to say to prompt him.

'Moved here with her man,' said Mr Harris, a frown

A FRESH START ON CRUMCAREY

marring his usually placid features. 'He's long-gone now, though. I don't know all the details…'

Luke raised his eyebrows at that. He'd *never* known a time when his uncle didn't have all the details! He stayed quiet, waiting for him to fill the silence.

'The idiot said he'd be back. Never has been, though,' he added.

'Back from where?' said Luke.

'Here, there and everywhere, from what I gather,' said Mr Harris. 'That card she had this morning? That would have been from him. He took a job on the mainland, and they started sending him all over the world.'

'And he just left her here… waiting for him?' said Luke.

'That's how I understand it,' said Mr Harris. 'I'm surprised she's still here – and good for her. She does her best, and she's done quite a lot of work on her own…'

'It's not going to last another winter,' said Luke, staring back at the sad little cottage. 'That roof's going to disappear at the slightest bit of wind. Those tarps aren't going to help if the cross beam goes…'

Honk!

The obnoxious blaring of a car horn made the pair of them jump. McGregor – rudely awoken from his nap – jumped to his feet and started barking and snarling at the window. His wiry fur stood on end as he glared at a campervan as it shot past them, overtaking at speed on the narrow road.

'You know, I swear he'd have two fingers up at them if he had fingers,' chuckled Luke, glancing at the little dog.

'Well deserved,' huffed Mr Harris.

'To be fair, we *are* stationary in the middle of the road,' said Luke, putting the truck in gear. With one last look at Maggie's cottage, he put his foot down. He needed to get back to the farm… he had some serious thinking to do.

CHAPTER 5

MAGGIE

It was getting dark... not because it was particularly late, but because one of those mad, blustery storms was heading up from the highlands towards Crumcarey.

The clouds had been gathering all afternoon. Now they were hanging in the sky - dense and heavy - as Maggie wound her way home from her first day at The Tallyaff.

Pulling off the road, Maggie made the executive decision to ease the car as far as she could get it inside the little lean-to garage at the side of the cottage. There were no doors on it, and the back of the space was piled high with boxes and old furniture that had been broken during the house move. Still, at least the walls on either side would give her a bit of shelter. With any luck, she'd be able to climb out of the car without losing a door in the process.

The wind was really ramping up, and Maggie had heard all sorts of horror stories about unsuspecting drivers losing control of their car doors in a storm. One gust and they could bend right back... or worse, catch an unsuspecting hand or leg! She could really do without having to find the money for car repairs right now. As for *Maggie* repairs... well... at least a stay in the hospital would mean a break from the constant DIY and tarpaulin-wrangling.

Speaking of which, she should really take a moment to do the rounds and check the tarps were all in place and secure before the storm got any closer. It was something she did as a matter of course every evening – checking the ropes and re-tying anything that looked like it was coming loose. It usually took her about twenty minutes... but judging by the colour of the sky and the fact the wind was busy turning her heavy plait into a lethal weapon, she didn't have time. She needed to hurry up and get inside!

'How bad can it be?' she sighed, glancing up at the roof and then instantly regretting her choice of words. It had been okay when she'd checked it the previous evening... or at least, as okay as it got. That didn't mean anything though.

Either way, she was shattered after her first shift, and she just wanted to cook some food and put her feet up. She'd simply have to deal with any damage in the morning.

Yawning widely, Maggie made her way inside,

turning on the lights as she went. They flickered a couple of times and she crossed her fingers that the trip switch wasn't going to get up to its usual shenanigans this evening. Ever since Russell had decided to "improve" the electrics, they'd been tripping left, right and centre. It wasn't really that surprising, considering there were still wires and dead ends dangling from the walls in every direction.

Russell had promised her that he'd left everything completely safe – safer than it had been to start with - but Maggie still made it a policy not to go near any of the dangling tangles of wire if she could help it. Sorting out the electrics was one of the many things on her to-do scroll – though she wasn't daft enough to think she'd be able to take on this particular job herself.

'Okay. We have light. Phew!' she breathed as they mercifully stopped flickering.

Maggie grabbed her torch off the hall shelf on her way past anyway – just in case. She knew from bitter experience it was better to have it somewhere nearby than bashing around in the pitch-black cottage searching for it. That was a guaranteed recipe for stubbed toes and bruised elbows!

Kicking off her pumps as she made her way through the open plan living room into the kitchen, Maggie wished – not for the first time – that she had something a bit more cosy on the floor than patches of bare boards and concrete. A snuggly sheepskin rug wouldn't go amiss right now. If someone had told her before she moved to Crumcarey that she'd have dreams about carpet that bordered on the erotic, she'd have laughed in their face.

Carpets...

Lino...

Shagpile!

'Idiot!' she chuckled, plonking her bag of groceries down onto the rickety bit of worktop next to the sink. Working at The Tallyaff was definitely going to have some perks – one of them being that she got first dibs on the fresh deliveries when they arrived.

Maggie had just started to unpack the bag of veg when a flapping growl from overhead made her flinch.

That didn't sound good!

She'd bet anything that was one of the tarps shifting... or maybe even blowing loose!

Moving to glance out of the window, Maggie craned her neck and stared upwards. Sure enough, she could just make out a corner of tarpaulin flapping wildly in the wind. Beyond it, the sky had grown even darker. As she watched, huge splatters of rain dashed against the single remaining pane of glass.

Okay – so it had officially been an awful idea not to check everything over. There was no way she was going out there now, though. It would be dangerous to head outside with the wind ramping up like that. She'd just have to ride it out.

How bad could it be, after all?

'Okay, stop saying – or *thinking* - that!' she gasped,

as another gust of wind shook the remaining roof slates.

'Deep breath,' she said, doing her best to keep calm. There wasn't any point getting worked up. This was what the weather was like here on Crumcarey. It was temperamental, loud, and its bark was usually worse than its bite.

Giving herself a little shake, Maggie continued to unload her shopping. She might be tired, but she'd promised herself that she'd cook a decent meal for once. Sure, she'd made the promise back around lunchtime… before her feet had started throbbing from wearing the unaccustomed flat pumps. She was really going to have to invest in a pair of decent trainers. Working at The Tallyaff definitely counted as some kind of endurance sport!

'Come on, Mags,' she yawned, grabbing a chopping board and choosing one of the onions. 'No tinned soup for you this evening!'

She had to admit, she'd been practically living off tinned food for months now. It was easy, quick and had the added bonus that it didn't spoil if the roof leaked on it. It didn't *quite* have the cosy, self-care vibe of a home-cooked meal though.

Maggie was just wiping away the first few tears from the decidedly pungent onion when the lights overhead started to flicker again.

'Noo no no no!' she gasped. 'Stop it!'

As if by magic, the cottage seemed to be listening.

Everything outside went still, and calm, and the lights behaved themselves as though nothing untoward had just happened.

'That's more like i—'

Maggie didn't even get to the end of the sentence before she was plunged into darkness.

'Aw crap,' she muttered. 'Perfect. Just perfect.'

All was not lost, though. She had her torch on the kitchen table. She'd use that to get the emergency candles lit. There was a two-ringed camping stove in the corner, and that ran on a little canister of gas. She'd have this curry if it was the last thing she did!

'Torch…' she muttered, feeling her way for the table and congratulating herself for bringing it through with her. She clicked the button, and the kitchen was briefly illuminated by the weak beam before it faded into nothingness.

'Don't you start!' muttered Maggie, giving the torch a hearty shake and clicking the button several times. It came back on for all of two seconds and then died.

Now that she thought about it - she'd meant to buy some new batteries.

Maggie took a deep breath. It would be fine. She'd just make her way over to her little wood burner and get that going. That would give her enough of a glow to light the candles and then…

Boom! Crash!! Shreddddd! SNAP!!

Maggie flinched, almost dropping the useless torch as the wind made a comeback at triple-strength. She didn't think she was imagining it – that had been something tearing from the roof – hadn't it?

Ducking her head instinctively, Maggie made her way across the room towards the wood burner with her hands outstretched, praying she didn't trip over anything.

'Gah!'

Crash!

This time it wasn't the roof, but one of the buckets she'd set out that morning to catch the drips. She'd just sent it flying across the room, and goodness only knows where it had landed.

Well… she'd just have to deal with that later. First, she needed some light!

Maggie's fingers found the smooth, curved surface of the metal flue that ran up the inside of the wall and sank to her knees in front of the cold fireplace. She cringed as another gust of wind crashed around the roof.

Groping around on the hearthstone, Maggie muttered curses under her breath until her fingers wrapped around the slender form of the long, clicky gas-match. Thanking her lucky stars that she'd already laid the fire, she opened the little door and gave the lighter a shake before clicking the button.

Nothing.

'Don't do this to me!' she muttered, clicking it again. It sparked, but there was no resulting flame. This *really* wasn't the time to run out of gas!

'Come on come on come on come on!' she chanted, clicking the button again and again.

Three minutes later, she had a sore thumb and still no fire...

CRASH!

With a whimper, Maggie turned in the dark and crawled in the direction of the sofa. As soon as her forehead bumped against its squashy edge, she climbed up and pulled an ancient throw blanket from the back, yanking it right up to her chin.

She stared around at the pitch darkness with wide eyes.

There had been plenty of times she'd been more than happy to be on her own in this cottage – and proud of it, in fact. Right now, though, she'd give anything for a bit of company... or a hug.

Covering her ears with her hands, Maggie screwed her eyes closed and - just for a moment - wished she was on that beach with the palm trees. In the background, there was a posh hotel waiting for her... a soft towelling robe... room service... Russell...

'No. Not that,' she said, her eyes flying open again.

She was happy here without him. He'd more than proven that he was the wrong person for her. She was just feeling sorry for herself because she was over-tired, hungry and a little bit scared.

Plus, the memory of Luke's lovely eyes and grubby hands – and how good he'd looked in a pair of overalls

– had done something strange to her brain... but she wasn't going to think about that right now.

'This too shall pass!' she said out loud, addressing the roof. It didn't sound particularly zen-like. Her voice was a bit too shrill for that, but it did make her bravery return a tiny bit.

She'd just stay put here on the sofa. The storm would ease, everything would calm down... and then she'd be able to do something about food... and light... and warmth... and...

CRASH!

The weight of the wind seemed to shake the entire cottage... but the resulting grinding, ripping and thudding wasn't the wind. It was something *far* more solid.

Maggie's hands automatically flew to her face with the shock, only for her to realise that there were tears on her cheeks.

Seriously? It had come to this?!

The backs of her hands were wet too.

Wait... what?!

'Uh oh!' she said, jumping out of the sofa and staring up at the roof... or... in this case, the clouds. The patch of slates directly above her head had disappeared, along with the tarpaulin that had been roped to them. Rain was falling thick and fast onto her face and the sofa.

'Not good! Not good!' she chanted, feeling her way to the end of the sofa and doing her best to shove it out from beneath the gaping hole. It was far too heavy, and she promptly gave up.

'Now what?' she muttered, doing her best to swallow the sob that was trying to choke her as she stared around.

Rain was falling inside her cottage – and not just where she was standing. That last gust had clearly removed most of her makeshift covers – and possibly a good chunk of the remaining slates too. There was no way it'd be safe for her to go outside and try to wrangle the tarpaulins back into place... not that she'd be able to find them, anyway... they'd probably be halfway to Denmark by now.

Maggie tried to take a deep breath, cowering as the storm raged overhead. She couldn't stay here. Not without power. Not without a roof!

The farm. It was her only option. She'd hop in the car and drive over to Mr Harris's to ask for help!

CHAPTER 6

LUKE

*L*uke loved the sound of the swirling wind and the rain clattering against the windowpanes. Nowhere else did storms quite like Crumcarey, and the wild weather running rampant outside while he was warm and cosy in his little barn made him feel decidedly at home.

Considering the place had been nothing more than a slightly scruffy blank canvas when he'd arrived, Luke was quite chuffed with the way it had turned out. It was amazing what a bit of a clear-out followed by a lick of paint could achieve. The empty space had transformed with the few bits of furniture he'd borrowed from his uncle's farmhouse. Of course, power and running water had definitely added to his creature comforts – which was exactly why they'd been at the top of his list of priorities.

Unfortunately, he hadn't quite managed to finish

the bathroom yet. Everything was in place – other than a bath. He had his eye on a gorgeous old roll-top affair, but right now, it was sitting in one of his uncle's fields, acting as the cows' water trough. Still... a bit of a scrub to get the green slime off and it would be as good as new!

For now, though, he had to resort to a strip wash... which was why he was currently stripped to the waist at the kitchen sink. It was warm out here with the wood burner blazing – so he didn't see the point in heading through to the bathroom!

Luke dipped his flannel into the bowl of scalding water and scrubbed at the sticky ooze that had somehow managed to coat his forearms. The real mystery was how it had made it onto the skin of his chest too. Considering he'd been wearing his overalls while he'd been helping Conner with a few bits on the ferry, he had no idea how it had got there. Perhaps he'd somehow managed to smear it across himself when he'd pulled his tee shirt over his head? Either way, it was proving an absolute nightmare to remove.

Yet again, the thick, oily substance threatened to glue the flannel to him rather than washing off. Luke sighed and grabbed the soap... and the scrubbing brush he kept on the windowsill. Desperate times called for desperate measures. If he could just scrub the worst of the stuff off without removing a layer of skin with it...

It didn't take long for his entire torso to get covered with frothy, sightly grimy suds.

'There – that must have done the trick!' he said, having endured several minutes of rather harsh brushing-action. Grabbing his flannel in his other hand, he sluiced some of the soap away.

'Hallelujah!' he grinned as the grime wiped away with it.

A hammering on the door of the barn made him turn in surprise. That didn't sound like the wind...

'Anyone in?' came a high-pitched voice that definitely *didn't* sound like his uncle. 'Help?'

In his haste to grab his towel, Luke fumbled with the soap-slick scrubbing brush and dropped it into the sink – getting a face full of sudsy water in return.

'Damn!' he spluttered, scrunching his eyes closed against the dripping, stinging water. He felt around blindly for his towel, but he couldn't find it.

'Help? Anyone home?!'

'Coming!' he called, giving up on the towel and doing his best to fist the water from his eyes as he hurried in the direction of the door.

Grabbing the handle, he threw it open and squinted out at a bedraggled shape. He couldn't really see much, what with the wind whipping at him and his soap-filled eyes. He brought his fists up again, doing his best to rub some sense into his eyeballs. Then he blinked... and the figure came into focus.

'Maggie?' he gasped.

'I'm sorry to bother you—' she started.

'Come inside!' he said, stepping out of the way and

beckoning for her to step in out of the storm. The minute she slipped past him, he closed the door firmly behind her.

'How can I help...' he turned to her, and his jaw dropped.

She wasn't just a little bit wet – she was soaked through. Her long hair hung over one shoulder just as it had earlier, but now a steady stream of water poured from it as if she'd just climbed out of a river rather than a car.

'Wait... did you *walk* here?' he gasped.

The beautiful, drowned rat in front of him nodded morosely as she continued to drip all over the floor. She looked done-in. A strange mixture of exhausted, completely resigned, and seriously close to tears.

'Are you hurt?' said Luke, as his confusion was nudged out of the way by his ever-present practical mode. If there was an accident on Crumcarey, time was of the essence – especially in a storm. It would be a nightmare to get the air ambulance out in weather like this.

'Not hurt,' muttered Maggie.

'Okay, good,' said Luke, silently instructing his rising panic to calm back down. 'Is anyone else hurt?' he added, just to be sure.

Maggie shook her head.

'And there's no fire?' he said.

Maggie snorted out a laugh that sounded like it

came from underwater. Or maybe it was a sob. It was hard to tell.

'Definitely no fire,' she said.

'Okay. Good,' said Luke.

'If you say so,' muttered Maggie.

Luke gave her a wry smile. 'I didn't mean *that* kind of fire.'

'I know,' she sighed. 'Sorry.'

'Just… stay there two secs,' said Luke, dashing through to the bathroom and grabbing the largest clean towel he could find.

'Thanks,' said Maggie as he handed it to her. She instantly wrapped it around the sodden length of her hair, doing her best to squeeze as much water from it as she could. Then she dried her face and glanced back up at him.

Luke bit his lip. Maggie looked like she'd just waded across the bottom of the sea from the mainland, and her mascara had trickled onto her cheeks… and yet she was breath-taking. He was having a hard time tearing his stinging eyes away from her.

'I'm sorry… I seem to have caught you at a bad moment?' she said.

Luke snapped to attention, realising that she seemed to be having exactly the same problem. He wasn't particularly big-headed, but he could swear her eyes had been glued to his chest two seconds ago.

'Ah… not… not bad,' he mumbled, beckoning for her to follow him into the kitchen.

Tee shirt. Where was his damn tee shirt?

He scuttled around, looking for the clean top he'd brought with him for after his wash and doing his best not to meet Maggie's eyes as she stood there, still rubbing her hair with the towel. He'd quite like to grab that towel and do the job for her. She needed to get out of those wet clothes too…

Speaking of clothes!

He grabbed his soft black tee shirt that had slipped onto the seat of one of his pilfered kitchen chairs and yanked it over his head.

There, that was better!

'Right,' he said. 'Sorry about that! Now… how can I help?'

'It's my roof,' she said in a small voice.

'Uh huh?' said Luke. He had a bad feeling he knew what was coming next.

'I think it's blown away.'

The words were met by a howling whistle from outside as the wind gusted around the outside of the barn's walls. It sounded like it was celebrating.

'You don't look surprised,' said Maggie when he didn't say anything.

'Sorry,' said Luke with a small shrug. 'We drove past your place earlier, and I saw that you've obviously been having… erm… a few issues!'

A small smile appeared on Maggie's face, and Luke pulled out a chair in response. He needed to sit down before his knees gave way.

'Understatement of the century, there,' said Maggie.

Luke shrugged. 'So… the tarps have blown off?'

'Erm… I think it's a bit worse than that,' said Maggie. 'And you don't look surprised… again.'

'I guess I'm not,' said Luke. 'Once these old roofs with the huge heavy slates start to fail, it doesn't take much for the rest to give way. And this storm… is… a lot! What I *am* surprised by, though, is that you walked here. Not sure that was the wisest choice if I'm honest.'

'I didn't get much choice in the matter,' said Maggie, pulling out the chair across from him and sliding into it.

'Car troubles?' said Luke.

'If that's what you call half your roof landing on half your car, then yes,' said Maggie.

'Oh,' said Luke. 'Shit.'

'Yep. It is a bit,' said Maggie. 'And as it's currently raining *inside* my house almost as much as it is outside… I thought I'd better come for some help.'

'Good call!' said Luke, nodding, though he had no idea what he could do to help with the weather still raging outside like an angry teenager. 'Erm… well… there's no way we can do anything about your roof in the pitch dark and in this weather.'

'No,' said Maggie. 'Definitely not.'

'Okay. Well… as far as I can see, you've got two options,' he said. 'One – we can make a dash for the truck, and I can drive you over to The Tallyaff. The road's going to be a bit of a mess... but we *should* make it over there in one piece...'

'As long as no one else's roof's flying about,' said Maggie.

'Yeah... there is that,' said Luke.

'What's option two?' said Maggie.

'You could stay the night here,' he said, wondering why the back of his neck was suddenly prickling.

Luke suddenly wished he wasn't sitting down. He felt like he needed to be on his feet – pacing – or at least doing something.

'I mean, you'd be slumming it!' he added quickly. 'This definitely isn't the Ritz! But I was about to start making some food, and there's a bottle of wine hiding around here somewhere. I think I left it in the bath.'

'The bath?' she laughed.

'It's not technically a bath yet,' he said. 'As in... there's no tub. I've just got a box sitting where a bath *will* be... and I think it's in there.'

It was a ridiculously long explanation for a ridiculous topic, but somehow, Luke felt like he needed to keep talking just to delay her inevitable request to be driven over to the Tally. He wasn't looking forward to that drive, and not just because the weather was so grim.

'Okay,' he said, forcing himself not to let out a sigh when she didn't speak for several long seconds. 'Okay...' he started to get to his feet. He'd need to put something warmer on if he had to go out in the storm. And some wellies…

'I'll stay here with you.'

Maggie's quiet voice stopped him in his tracks.

'If you're sure that's okay?'

Okay?

'Sure.' *Do not start grinning like an idiot. Do not air punch.* 'That's okay with me.'

CHAPTER 7

MAGGIE

Maggie blinked.
Had she really said that?
She couldn't believe she'd had the balls.

Maybe she was still in shock from the walk? If she was being honest, it had been more like a crawl – the wind had simply been too strong for anything else. It had been very wet, very loud and very scary – a true sensory overload.

By the time she'd reached Luke's door, there had been tears mingling with the rainwater dripping from her face. With any luck, the gorgeous guy across the table from her might not have noticed. Then again… she didn't really care if he had. She had nothing to prove… did she?!

Either way, her rather firm decision to stay put had everything to do with not wanting to head back out into the storm, and nothing at all to do with the opportunity to hang out here with a gorgeous man in his lovely, cosy home. If she kept telling herself that, she might eventually believe it.

Was it worth turning down The Tallyaff – where there was carpet, and a bar… and probably even a bath that worked? Absolutely.

'I like what you've done with the place,' she said, glancing around at the clean walls, simple furniture and twinkling golden lights.

How had he turned this old cow shed into a home in just a few short weeks?

'Thanks,' said Luke, running his fingers through his hair and looking a little bit lost. 'Had you seen inside before?'

Maggie shook her head. She'd definitely seen the building from the outside though. Russell had always slowed down whenever they'd driven past Mr Harris's farm. He'd enjoyed sneering at the state of the place and crowing about the fact that the old farmer was bound to ask him for help once he saw what a beautiful job he was going to do at Pear Tree Cottage.

'What did my place used to be called?'

The question popped out of Maggie's mouth before she'd realised that her brain had wandered down a random rabbit hole.

'Brae Byre,' said Luke, cocking his head curiously. 'At least, that's what Uncle Harris told me.'

'Better than bloody Pear Tree Cottage,' she huffed.

'Where's that?' said Luke, looking confused.

'That's what it's called now,' said Maggie, a weight of weariness suddenly descending on her. 'My cottage, I mean. That's what Russell – my ex – wanted to call it.'

He'd been getting job offers left right and centre at that point, so she'd just gone along with it. He'd been turning them all down, and she hadn't wanted to give him any reason to take the offers a bit more seriously. She'd wanted to keep him sweet… she hadn't wanted him to disappear on her. A fat lot of good it did her!

'Ah… that explains why Uncle Harris was muttering something about "no trees" when we drove past!' said Luke with a small smile. 'I don't think there's a pear tree closer than about two hundred miles south of here. Pretty name, though,' he added quickly.

'Stupid name,' she huffed, shaking her head. 'Sorry.'

'What are you apologising for?!' said Luke, looking surprised.

'For ruining your evening because my stupidly named cottage no longer has a roof.'

Maggie was aware that her voice had taken on a whiney edge – but for a brief moment, she couldn't bring herself to care. She was sitting in a barn that had been turned into a cosier home than hers in just three weeks. It was warm, dry and clean. It was all the things her place wasn't. Plus, she was tired and cold, and all that was waiting for her back at stupid Pear Tree Cottage was less than half a roof, a squashed car and some death-trap wiring.

Maggie shivered.

'Okay – it's time to get you out of those wet clothes,' said Luke. 'In the nicest way possible!' he added quickly. 'I didn't mean…'

'It's okay,' said Maggie, forcing a smile. 'And that would be good…' She trailed off, wrapping her arms around herself in a vain attempt to warm up a bit, but there was no way that was going to happen while she was wearing several layers of sodden clothes.

'I haven't got much in the way of clothes for you to change into… at least, not ones that'll fit!' he said. 'I do have some clean tee shirts though… and there's a fresh pair of overalls – at least they won't keep falling down on you!'

'Yes please,' she said. Anything had to be better than wet skinny jeans!

Luke ambled over to an alcove behind his settee and rummaged in a drawer, pulling out various bits and pieces until he found what he was looking for.

'Here,' he said, holding the mercifully dry clothing out towards her. 'You can change in the bathroom – it's just through there,' he pointed at a door on the other side of the room.

Maggie nearly swooned at the sight. A bathroom that had a door *and* a working handle? She'd clearly died and gone to heaven.

'Thanks,' she said, shooting him a grateful smile.

'Take your time,' he said with a little nod.

Maggie's stomach flipped, and for a brief moment, she had the almost uncontrollable urge to wrap her arms around Luke and cuddle the living daylights out of him.

'Be right back!' she squeaked, making a dash for the bathroom.

Closing the door behind her, Maggie did her best to take a deep breath and will her racing heart to calm down. Not easy when she was standing in a bathroom with a working light *and* running water! *Heaven!*

Dashing to the sink, Maggie turned the hot tap on and gasped. Hot... running... water. It was pure luxury! Sure, the pipework was exposed and there weren't any tiles on the walls or floor yet, but the old stone walls had been beautifully re-pointed. There wasn't a single cobweb to be seen in the corners... and there was no sign of green algae growing on the window frame. Unlike some *other* places she could mention.

'I'm moving in,' she whispered, taking everything in.

Just as Luke had said, there was a large space where the bath should be. The copper piping simply came to an abrupt halt on the wall, and there was a pipe that peeped up through the floorboards, awaiting its time to shine.

Instead of a bath, there were a couple of familiar-looking plastic boxes filled with an array of jars, bottles and other assorted bits and pieces. Maggie spotted the bottle of wine Luke had mentioned and smiled.

First things first, though.

Reaching behind her, Maggie grabbed her sopping-wet jumper and struggled to peel it up over her head.

For a moment, it seemed to get wedged, and she sucked in a long, slow breath as she did her best to stay calm inside her slightly gross prison. It wasn't easy when suddenly all she could think about was what Luke had looked like when she'd arrived. Topless. Tanned. Delicious.

A chill ran down Maggie's spine. Or maybe it was up? She couldn't work out which way it was travelling because it seemed to be everywhere all at once.

'Idiot!' she muttered, finally managing to drag the top over her head. Undoing her belt with cold, shaking fingers, she began to wrestle her way out of the stiff, soggy denim of her drenched jeans. *Yuck!*

No… she wouldn't linger on how good Luke had looked, still slightly damp, with soap bubbles on his chin. She didn't know anything about him. As nice as he looked… and as nice as he seemed… men just weren't on her agenda right now.

'Won't hurt to get to know him, though,' she whispered, turning to glance in a small mirror that was propped up above the washbasin. 'Oh no!' she gasped, spotting dark smudges where her mascara had melted down her face. She should have known, given the fact that she'd basically bathed in rain *and* tears on her way over. It wasn't like she ever wore bloomin' mascara, either. She'd only put some on in an attempt to look a little bit less *unkempt* for her first day at work!

Maggie stuffed the plug into the sink and ran some hot water into the basin. Then she used her cupped hands to rinse her face, revelling in the delicious warmth, before grabbing her already-damp towel and using one corner to wipe away the worst of the mascara smudges.

Giving her hair another vigorous rub, she did her best to comb it out with her fingers before pulling it into a plait. Then she twisted it into a bun for good measure, securing the whole lot with a hairband. She doubted Luke would have a hairdryer lying around, so at least this would stop it from instantly making a wet patch on her lovely dry clothes.

'Hey Maggie?'

The light knock on the door made her jump.

'Yeah?' she squeaked, grabbing the towel and holding it up to her front as though Luke might barge his way in. Which – of course – was stupid!

'When you're done, could you grab that bottle of wine?' he said. 'I think you've earned a glass!'

'Okay!' she said, her voice coming out ridiculously high and quivery. 'Will do!'

Wine might not be the best plan considering her less-than-stable emotions right now... but she hadn't had a glass in ages. Frankly, after the day she'd just had... why not?

CHAPTER 8

LUKE

Luke did his best not to look as Maggie reappeared from the bathroom. She hadn't quite finished buttoning up her overalls, and there was a tantalising glimpse of soft skin on display. He didn't want to be *that* guy. She'd come to him for help, and there was no way he was up for doing anything that might make her feel any more uncomfortable than she already was.

Instead, he focussed on finishing chopping up some ginger and scraping it into the already-sizzling onions in the pan sitting on his little countertop hob. He might not have an oven yet, but it was amazing what you could do with four rings at your disposal.

'Something smells good!'

Maggie's soft voice close behind him made him look up again, and he was both relieved and a bit disappointed to discover that she'd clearly noticed and rectified the open-popper issue. Luke cleared his throat and made a show of rubbing his eyes on his sleeve – as though the cooking onions were to blame for his gaze drifting out of his control.

'Nothing fancy, I'm afraid,' he said. 'Just a bit of a stir fry and some rice – hope that's okay for you?'

'Sounds brilliant!' she said, and Luke breathed a sigh of relief to hear genuine enthusiasm in her voice. 'Here's the wine,' she added, giving the bottle a little waggle. 'Anything I can do to help?'

'I've already dug out the corkscrew,' he said, motioning with his head to the newly installed drainer by the kitchen sink. 'If you wouldn't mind doing the honours?'

'I'm on it!' said Maggie.

'I'm afraid I don't have wine glasses,' he said quickly. 'Best I can do is those jam jars.'

'Hey – I'm not knocking it!' said Maggie, and he could hear the warmth of a smile in her voice even though he couldn't actually see her. 'You have wine… that's way more than I brought. I don't care what we drink it out of!'

Luke focused on chopping the mound of veg in front of him, all the while fighting the urge to turn and just stare at the beautiful woman in his kitchen. This day had taken a very weird turn indeed. He almost felt like he'd conjured Maggie up… he *had* been thinking about her non-stop since breakfast at The Tallyaff, after all.

'How was your first day?' he asked, glad to have stumbled on a topic of conversation that felt relatively safe. Luke didn't know much about Maggie, other than the fact that she had a dumbass ex who'd basically abandoned her here on Crumcarey, and a cottage that sounded very much like it was in the process of falling down around her ears. Neither of those topics shouted *light first-date conversation!*

Not that this was a first date.

At all.

Gah!

'It was great, thanks!' said Maggie, her voice pulling him back into the present and stopping him from heading any further into the hole he was busily digging for himself. 'My feet are killing me though,' she laughed. 'I'm not used to so much standing... or stairs! I've been up and down to the guest rooms that many times today, I lost count. I don't think I've had to climb stairs since I moved here. The cottage is like this – just the one floor.'

'I bet your feet will get used to it pretty quickly,' said Luke. 'But... why don't you sit while I sort the food out!'

'Not a chance,' she said, her smiling face appearing at his side. She placed his jam jar of wine down next to the chopping board. 'That's not how saving this particular damsel in distress works. What can I do to help?'

Luke grinned at her. He couldn't help it. 'You could make the sauce for this lot?'

'I'm on it! Have you got some soy sauce... sweet chilly?' she said, peering around at the decided lack of kitchen cupboards available to rummage through.

'There's a box of jars and bottles over there in the corner,' he said with a nod, as he started to finely slice a courgette into batons.

'So... to answer your question,' said Maggie, the box of condiments clinking as she began to rummage through them, 'other than my feet, today was brilliant. Olive's lovely – and there are so many visitors, there's no chance to get bored!'

'Urgh... the one thing I hate!' chuckled Luke. 'I prefer to keep busy.'

'Erm yeah... I can see that,' said Maggie.

He glanced over at her, only to find her staring around the open-plan space he currently called home with something a bit like wonder on her face. It made something strange and warm settle in his chest.

'So... how long exactly did it take you to get this place from barn to cosy cottage?' she said.

Luke paused in his chopping. 'About two weeks?' he said. 'I mean – I've been here for just over three, but I stayed a couple of nights in the farmhouse with Uncle Harris, until I realised that wasn't an option.'

'Why not?' said Maggie, sounding surprised.

'The snoring,' muttered Luke. 'Uncle reckons it's the dog, but considering you can hear their duet all the

A FRESH START ON CRUMCAREY

way over here... I'd say it's both of them. And let that be a warning for later - don't freak out if you hear something ominous in the middle of the night. It's just those two and their nose flutes!'

'Noted!' chuckled Maggie. 'Right, I've got mango chutney for sweetness, soy sauce... and a bit of actual chilly... have you got any cornflower?'

'Erm... nope?' said Luke apologetically. 'I'll grab some for next time, though.'

'Okay,' said Maggie.

Luke instantly wanted to kick himself. He'd just managed to invite her on a second date without meaning to! Not that this was a date... not that...

Shut up, Luke. Stop thinking... just cook!

As Maggie grabbed a clean jam jar from his stash and started to mix a sauce for the stir-fry, Luke couldn't quite believe how easy it was to have her in the cottage. She just seemed to get on with things – comfortable with the easy silence as they both concentrated on what they were doing. It was weird. He never usually felt this comfortable with another person in his space – especially not someone he'd only just met!

'You know... I'm really sorry to land on you like this and spoil your evening,' she said, popping the glass of mixed sauce down next to him and then taking a sip of her wine.

'I'm glad you did,' he said, happy that he was able to say it quite so truthfully. 'And you're definitely not spoiling my evening! There's no way I'd be up for you heading back to the cottage anyway. Not until this storm calms down and it's light enough to see what the damage is.'

Maggie nodded, looking anxious.

'And, for the record, I'm glad you chose to stay here instead of heading over to The Tallyaff. I wouldn't fancy getting caught out in that right now!'

The pair of them paused, listening to the wind as it howled around the farmyard.

'Yeah – that wouldn't have been a fun drive!' said Maggie. 'It's just…' she trailed off and Luke raised an eyebrow. The ease that had existed between them just a couple of minutes ago seemed to have evaporated.

'What is it?' said Luke in concern. 'Look, I totally get it. You don't know me. Maybe… how about after we've eaten, I could walk you up to the farmhouse. We can ask Uncle Harris if you can sleep there. I'm sure he won't mind. You know him better, and…'

'You wouldn't subject me to the nose flutes?!' gasped Maggie in mock horror.

'Only if you wanted,' said Luke.

'I definitely *don't* – thanks!' said Maggie with a small smile. 'As long as you don't mind me kipping on your sofa for the night, of course.'

'No chance,' said Luke firmly.

'Oh,' said Maggie. 'I get it… I mean, I—'

'You get the bed. I'll take the sofa.'

A FRESH START ON CRUMCAREY

'I couldn't possibly!' said Maggie. 'Don't worry – I'm not a princess.'

'You're taking the bed,' he said firmly. 'Either that, or you can walk home!'

He hadn't meant the last bit of course, and the storm seemed to be in on the joke as it chose that moment to grab hold of the front door and give it a good rattle.

'The bed sounds perfect!' said Maggie quickly, letting out an easy laugh.

Less than twenty minutes later, they both carried heaped bowls of slightly sloppy stir fry and rice over to the kitchen table. Maggie let out a sigh of relief as she finally sat down.

'Cheers!' she said, raising a forkful of food in his direction instead of her glass. 'Thanks for coming to my rescue.'

'Cheers!' said Luke, mirroring her and then stuffing the forkful into his face before he could say anything cheesy and spoil the moment.

CHAPTER 9

MAGGIE

The meal was unexpectedly delicious, especially considering she'd rather winged the sauce. It was a bit like a cross between stir-fry and soup… but the rice did a lovely job of soaking up all the juice. In fact, Maggie might even go so far as to say that she was enjoying it more than her much-anticipated curry… though she had a feeling that might have more to do with the sparkling company than anything else.

So far, their conversation had flowed easily – which was a bit of a wonder, considering she'd only met the man that morning. Whenever the topic strayed a bit close to something that made her fidget, Luke promptly headed it off in another direction without so much as a pause.

It didn't take long before Maggie felt completely relaxed… a miracle considering she'd appeared on his doorstep looking like a drowned rat less than an hour ago.

'So… what brought you to the island?' said Maggie, mopping up the last of her sauce with a crust of bread. 'Were you brought up here?'

Luke shook his head, sitting back in his chair and shooting a mournful glance at his empty bowl. 'No, I wasn't born here, but I do feel a bit like an honorary member of the community. I love Crumcarey… always have. It feels like coming home. The beginning of the summer was my favourite time of year when I was a kid. I'd travel up to stay with Uncle Harris… and I never wanted to go back down south at the end of the holidays.'

'I can imagine,' said Maggie with a smile. 'This place must be magical when you're little.'

'Lots of freedom,' said Luke with a nod. 'Everyone looks out for the bairns up here.'

'I like that,' said Maggie. 'And as an adult…?'

'I still love visiting Uncle Harris,' he laughed. 'Sometimes for longer, sometimes for shorter. I crewed the ferry one summer when I was in my twenties. Another year, I worked with Mr McCluskey on his fishing boat.'

'Anna's dad?' said Maggie. 'Who lives with Ray?'

'That's the one,' said Luke. 'You know… his boat was called Maggie too!'

Maggie grinned. She wasn't sure what to say to that. 'So, is this a longer visit or one of the shorter ones?'

'Not sure yet,' said Luke with an easy smile. 'My uncle's not getting any younger though, and I want to spend some time with him before I head off. I'm not sure what I'll do when the winter sets in… but I guess I'll figure that out when it gets here!'

Maggie nodded, doing her best to ignore the tiny squirm of discomfort at the idea of her new friend leaving the island so soon. How ridiculous could she get? After all… she'd only met him that morning!

Doing her best to shrug off the strange, mournful feeling, Maggie sat back in her chair and let out a sigh. The room was warm and cosy, and even though the rain was still beating on the roof and windows, the wind had eased off a tiny bit. She was full and snuggly, and her tiredness felt like it was draped around her shoulders like a blanket.

'Your turn,' said Luke. 'What brought you to Crumcarey?'

'You mean why am I living at the edge of the world in little more than a chicken shed?' she said with a yawn.

'You said it, not me!' he chuckled.

Maybe it was the warmth or the wine or the fact that she didn't really know Luke… but there didn't seem any point in *not* telling him the truth. She'd not really told anyone the full story before - mainly because she hadn't wanted to be judged by the locals. Stupid, really, considering they probably knew all the sordid details anyway. Nothing much escaped the Crumcarey gossip mill.

Maggie sighed again. She'd been silent for long enough. It was time to get it off her chest... she just hoped she could do it without sounding too bitter and twisted about the whole thing. After all, it wasn't Russell's fault. Not entirely, anyway!

'Well... we bought the cottage without viewing it first,' she said. It was hard to know where to start, but that was probably the most obvious place. Plus, it was the detail she was most worried about being judged for.

'Wow – that was brave!' said Luke, raising an eyebrow.

'Or stupid,' said Maggie.

'Brave,' repeated Luke, shaking his head. 'Had you been to Crumcarey before?'

It was Maggie's turn to shake her head.

'A real adventure then!'

Maggie smiled at him as the knot in her chest eased a little. Sure, things had gone sour after the move, but it *had* been an adventure at the time!

'I moved here originally with Russell – my boyfriend,' she said. 'My ex, I guess I should say.'

'Your ex?'

'Yeah,' she sighed. 'He left after about six months to take a job back on the mainland. We never officially split up, but...'

'Does he visit?' said Luke.

'Nope,' said Maggie, shaking her head. 'I mean, it's definitely over. I've not seen him or spoken to him for over a year, so…'

'Definitely over,' agreed Luke in a steady voice. 'And… does he own Pear Tree Cottage with you.'

'Actually, no!' said Maggie. 'I sold my flat down south and bought it outright with the proceeds. There was enough left over to live on while we worked on the place.'

Until recently, of course, but Luke didn't need to know the ins and outs of her slightly sorry finances!

'Well, at least that's something,' said Luke.

'Yeah,' she said, a little laugh slipping out as she said it. 'A little heap of something.'

'Don't count your slipped slates before the morning,' said Luke gently. 'It might have sounded worse than it actually was.'

'Tell that to my poor car!' said Maggie.

'Okay… yeah. Anyway – we'll sort it out one way or another, don't worry.'

'Thanks,' said Maggie, smiling at him gratefully. How could she not? The guy was single-handedly making her feel less alone than she had since Russell had left. Hell – since *before* Russell had left. Not that she *couldn't* deal with it on her own… it was just that for once, it was nice to feel like she might have the backup of another human being standing by her side.

'So you both made the move and started doing the place up?' prompted Luke.

Maggie couldn't help but pull a face. Luke had already told her that he'd clocked the state of the cottage on his way past, and she was pretty sure Olive and Mr Harris would have filled him in on the rest.

'Russell wasn't very… handy,' she said, doing her best to be diplomatic.

'Ah,' said Luke.

'Uh huh,' agreed Maggie.

'I bought lots of materials… and tools…' she continued. 'And I did my best to learn as much as I could as we went along. I learned even more after he left. We just… I just never seem to get very far with it.'

'Do you regret it?' said Luke. 'Moving here, I mean? Buying the cottage.'

Maggie shook her head. 'Nope. Not for a second. It was a risky decision – but I was up for the adventure. Russell might have turned out to be an arse, but I'm grateful to him for his mad plan… because it brought me here.'

'I like your attitude,' said Luke with a grin.

'I've had time to work on it,' she said with a wry smile. 'Either way, I could have sold up after Russell disappeared… but this is home now. Crumcarey is, I mean. I'm not so sure about Pear Tree Cottage. I *do* like it there… but it's going to take a lot of work.' She paused, feeling the blanket of weariness settle even heavier on her shoulders. 'If I'm honest, I'm not sure I've got the energy left. I've been working so hard just to stop the place from falling down… and now it kind of… has.'

'I get it,' said Luke. 'But everything will look better in the daylight. You'll see.'

'Everything looked better the minute you opened your door,' she said.

Luke smiled at her, shifting slightly in his seat.

'Erm… sorry!' she laughed. 'I've not had wine in a *very* long time.'

'Well then,' said Luke, lifting the bottle and tilting it towards her in an invitation. 'We'd better make up for that!'

CHAPTER 10

LUKE

Luke clambered to his feet and was surprised to find the room spinning gently around him. Blimey, the wine had hit him harder than he'd realised.

Grabbing his bowl from the table, he reached across for Maggie's with a slightly wonky smile. He got her full-wattage beam in return, and it nearly swiped his legs right out from beneath him.

Wow!

Luke forced himself to turn away before he did something stupid, and made his way slowly over towards the sink – willing the world to stop swaying as he went. Perhaps the wine hadn't been such a good idea after all!

'Man, I'm ready for some sleep!' he yawned, secretly wondering if he'd manage to get any with Maggie under the same roof.

'Amen!' she echoed, appearing at his side with the empty wine bottle and jam jars. 'Let me just do the washing up, and then—'

'Not a chance,' said Luke. 'There's not that much, anyway. I'll deal with it tomorrow.'

'Oh good,' chuckled Maggie, grinning up at him. The room spun even faster as his heartbeat did something peculiar. 'I was hoping you'd say that.'

'Playing a dangerous game there, Mags,' he said, naturally shortening her name and then wondering if perhaps he was taking liberties. Then he gave a mental shrug – he'd had too much wine to worry about it either way. 'I could have called your bluff and set you to work.'

'Nah, not your style,' said Maggie.

Luke beamed at her. He liked how that sounded – as though they'd known each other long enough for her to work out all his little foibles.

'Let's get some sleep,' he said. 'I can drive you over to the cottage in the morning if you'd like? We could take a look at the damage before you have to head into work…?'

Every fibre of his being wanted to declare that she had nothing to worry about – that no matter what state the place was in, he'd help. He'd take over and make everything right for her. But even in his slightly befuddled state, he knew that was the last thing she needed.

Maggie was clearly an independent soul. From

what he could gather, today was the first time she'd asked for - or accepted - any kind of assistance since she'd moved to Crumcarey.

Baby steps.

He'd work out a way to give her a hand... but there was no way he was going to make her feel stomped all over. It sounded like she'd had quite enough of that with her ex.

'That would be great,' said Maggie. 'Thanks. Now... are you sure about me having the bed?'

Luke watched her as she glanced around the barn. He had a feeling it was only just dawning on her that the place was completely open-plan – kitchen, living room and bedroom all rolled into one. The bed was tucked away in the far corner, but the only truly private place in his little home was the bathroom.

'I'm sure!' he said. 'The sofa's pretty comfy... and I'm used to it. I only built the bed base a week ago. Also, there's a curtain you can pull around it. I put it up to help keep the draft out... but it'll give you a bit of privacy.'

'Oh – cool,' she said. 'Okay, thanks.'

Luke saw her swallow. He couldn't quite work out if she was feeling nervous, knackered, guilty for making him sleep on the sofa... or a mixture of all three.

'Here,' he said, reaching for a clean jam jar and filling it from the cold tap. 'You might need this in the night... after the wine!'

'Ta,' she said, taking it from him.

'Oh… and do you want to hang your wet things on the rack around the wood burner before bed, too?' he added, kicking himself for not suggesting it earlier. 'They should be nice and dry by the morning.'

'That'd be great!' she said, popping her water down on the table. 'I'll just grab them?'

Luke nodded and watched her make a dash for the bathroom before turning to stoke up the fire. Then, he closed it back to keep going through the night and set up his wooden clothes racks around it.

Straightening up, Luke cast a longing look at his bed. He was quite pleased with how it had turned out. Mr Harris had given him the mattress – which had barely been used – and Luke had built the base using rafters from one of the old barns. The roof had fallen in years ago and now it was just used as a sheltered spot for growing rhubarb.

Luke didn't mind sleeping on the sofa one little bit… but he'd love nothing more than to curl up with Maggie under the covers and doze off to the sounds of the crackling wood burner.

Shaking his head to dislodge the rogue thought, Luke started to shift the cushions around on the sofa.

'All sorted?' he asked, looking up as Maggie re-emerged from the bathroom.

'It's all yours. I snaffled a bit of your toothpaste,' said Maggie with a smile, holding her pile of wet clothes at arm's length. 'Don't worry… I used my finger, not your brush!'

'Grand,' said Luke. 'Erm… I've put a pair of my boxers and another tee shirt on the bed… for you to sleep in.' He paused, suddenly wondering if that particular move was a bit weird. Maybe he'd managed to go one step too far in his wine-fuelled haze. 'They're clean!'

'Oh,' said Maggie, biting her lip and looking like she was having a hard time not giggling. 'Great. Thanks.'

'Night then,' said Luke. 'I'm just going to use the bathroom and I'll grab the lights on my way back.'

'Okay… okay,' said Maggie. 'Erm… night Luke. And – thank you.'

Luke grinned at her. It didn't feel like enough. He wanted to kiss her… on the cheek… or… somewhere else. Maybe he should at least give her a hug?

No, maybe not!

Instead, Luke gave her a strange, stiff salute then rolled his eyes and shot off towards the bathroom before he could make any more of a prat out of himself.

CHAPTER 11

MAGGIE

Maggie lay as stiff as a board. Her muscles were coiled, and she was ready to bolt upright at the slightest sound of movement.

It wasn't the bed's fault. It was warm and cosy, and she'd love nothing more than to curl up in an exhausted ball and float off to sleep underneath the soft mound of blankets. But... until those lights went out and she heard Luke settle on the sofa, she was on high alert.

It wasn't because she didn't feel safe – because she did – absolutely. She might not know him very well, but she trusted Luke. Even so... there was something in the air she couldn't quite put her finger on.

Possibility.

A spark of electricity.

She didn't think she was imagining it.

She *hoped* she wasn't imagining it.

Of course, it didn't help that she was surrounded by the scent of Luke. Warm, spicy. Delicious.

Maggie wriggled her toes.

The room suddenly went dark, and she strained her ears to catch the sound of Luke's padding footsteps as he made his way over to the sofa. There was a creak, the rustle of a duvet being pulled up to a bristly chin, and then complete silence other than the crackling of the wood burner and the sound of rain still beating against the roof.

'Night Luke,' she whispered into the darkness of her little curtained cave.

'Night Mags,' came a soft whisper from across the room.

Maggie turned onto her side and grinned into the pillow as she finally relaxed in the cosy warmth of the bed. Reaching out, she pushed the curtain aside. The dim flicker of the wood burner's flames danced on the whitewashed walls. It was barely enough to illuminate the space, but she could just make out the outline of the sofa, and the soft mound of duvet nestled in its depths.

Maggie knew she should feel weird, invading someone else's bed like this. Hell, the whole evening should have been weird. That couldn't be further from the truth, though. She felt strangely at home in Luke's company. As for this little barn… it was exactly what she'd hoped Pear Tree Cottage would have turned into by now.

Maggie frowned a little at the thought.

When she'd first arrived on Crumcarey, she hadn't minded the idea of camping at the cottage for a couple of years while they got the jobs done one by one. But… that had come with a couple of caveats. Things had to be moving in the right direction – and at the very least, she wanted to be warm and dry.

Was it so unreasonable that those were her bare minimum requirements before she'd agreed to the whole thing? She certainly didn't think so.

Of course, the reality of Pear Tree Cottage had turned into something else entirely – a slow, messy nightmare. Luke's barn was the way it *should* have been… and it had only taken him a couple of weeks to achieve it.

Amazing.

Who knew what state the cottage would be in by the time the storm finally blew itself out. What if she couldn't even live there anymore?! No matter what Luke had said earlier about the damage sounding worse than it actually was - he hadn't been there when it had happened. He hadn't seen the vast tangle of tarp and roof slates that had dumped themselves onto her poor little car!

Maggie felt her chin quiver and she quickly shifted to lie on her other side, facing the wall. It might be dark and there might be a curtain, but she wasn't going to show this moment of weakness to the world.

Taking a deep breath, Maggie did her best to steady herself.

Maybe Luke was right... maybe everything would feel better in the morning... maybe...

Letting out a long, slow sigh, Maggie's eyes fluttered closed as Luke's sweet, spicey scent eased her off to sleep.

~

Maggie yawned widely and opened her eyes... only to find herself staring at an unfamiliar, whitewashed stone wall.

Huh?!

Her bed didn't smell right. And... what on earth was she wearing?!

It took a couple of seconds for reality to dawn on her. When it did, she settled back with a grin. Luke's bed. Luke's tee shirt. Luke's bloomin' boxer shorts!

A little snort of laughter escaped her, and she clapped her hand over her mouth. She had no idea what time it was, and she didn't want to wake Luke if he was still conked out on the sofa.

Yawning widely, Maggie stared idly up at the ceiling for a long moment. That had to have been the deepest, most restful sleep she'd had in months... which was a bit of a miracle, given the reason behind her flight through the storm to Luke's barn in the first place.

The thought dragged her fully out of sleep, and she

struggled to sit up. Grabbing the edge of the curtain surrounding her little corner, she peeped around it, only to find the sofa had been abandoned. The duvet was on the floor, and sounds of splashing drifted over from the direction of the bathroom.

So – Luke was awake too. Perfect!

Jumping out of bed, Maggie made a beeline for her clothes. With any luck, they'd be nice and dry, and she'd be able to make a dash back to her bed-cave before poor old Luke was treated to the sight of her creeping around in his boxers.

With a quick glance over her shoulder to make sure the coast was clear, Maggie felt one leg of her jeans. The denim was rough and stiff – but mercifully dry! She was just gathering the rest of her clothes into her arms when the front door of the barn flew open, making her jump.

'Oh!' said Mr Harris, his bushy eyebrows bristling as he stared at her in surprise.

Didn't the man knock?!

Of course he didn't - it *was* his farm after all!

'Morning!' came a cheerful voice from the other side of the room.

Oh great!

Maggie's eyes flew from Mr Harris to Luke and then down to the scruffy, wiry little dog who'd just pelted towards her and was now busy licking her ankles.

'Blimey Mags – he likes you!' chuckled Luke.

Maggie met his eye for a split second, her face turning a steaming pink.

'I… didn't mean to intrude…' said Mr Harris, looking confused as he eyed Maggie's makeshift pyjamas. He threw a questioning glance at Luke and then turned back to her.

'We can explain!' said Maggie.

Luke snorted with laughter.

Maggie had to rein in the temptation to stick her tongue out at him. She couldn't blame him though – she *was* doing a very good impression of a teenager caught red-handed after sneaking into a boy's room!

'Why don't you get dressed and I'll put the kettle on?' said Luke, clearly taking pity on her.

'Clothes. Good idea,' said Mr Harris, nodding. 'You might give poor old McGregor a heart attack.'

Luke started to giggle, and Maggie gave in and stuck her tongue out at him before dashing back to the bed and closing the curtain firmly behind her. It didn't stop a snuffly little nose from making its way underneath the edge two seconds later.

'McGregor!' the two men shouted in unison, and the terrier disappeared with what she could swear was a roll of his beady little eyes.

Maggie started to pull her clothes on as fast as she could.

'Here,' said Luke, handing her a steaming vat of coffee the minute she reappeared.

'Ta,' she said, wrapping her hands gratefully around the gigantic mug and taking a sip.

'So. Are either of you going to tell me what on earth I've just walked in on?' said Mr Harris.

Maggie grinned at him, feeling a bit less exposed now that she was back in her own clothes.

'I'm afraid my cottage had a little accident in the storm,' she said.

'How little?' said Mr Harris, looking concerned.

'Most of the roof kind of little?' she said.

'Oh dear,' he said.

'Yeah,' said Maggie, feeling a dollop of dread drop into her stomach.

'To be fair, we've not had the chance to have a proper look yet,' said Luke mildly.

Maggie smiled at him gratefully. He was clearly trying to stop her from running away with herself before they'd had the chance to assess the damage.

'Anyway,' said Maggie, 'I didn't know what to do, so I came over here... you guys are the closest.'

'You're always welcome,' said Mr Harris seriously. 'Where's your car, though – I didn't see it?'

'Underneath most of the roof,' said Maggie.

'Oh dear,' said Mr Harris again. 'Well... that *does* explain why there are several tarpaulins and a bunch of snapped rope up in the top field!'

'Oh no, I'm so sorry,' said Maggie.

'Don't you apologise, girl!' said Mr Harris, shaking his head. 'I was just on my way down to find Luke to help me collect it all up. Then I was going to drive over to the cottage to make sure you're alright.'

'I'm alright,' said Maggie. 'Thank you, though.'

'A miracle you are, too,' said Mr Harris.

'Yeah, especially as she practically swam here last night!' said Luke, his voice serious.

McGregor – who'd been sitting on Maggie's foot while all this had been going on – glanced up at her and barked. It sounded very much like he was telling her off.

'Consider yourself told!' laughed Luke. 'But that reminds me – I've put fresh batteries in this for you.'

Maggie took the torch from him. She had no idea why she'd brought it with her, considering it had been as dead as a dodo and about as much use as a chocolate teapot.

'Thank you,' she said, giving him a tiny smile.

'Well… now there are two of you to help me tidy up the field,' said Mr Harris. 'Drink that coffee up… we've got work to do.'

CHAPTER 12

LUKE

Luke trudged towards his uncle's pickup and then held the door open for Maggie. He waited as she clambered up into the centre seat before making his way around to the driver's side.

'Who said you could drive?' muttered Mr Harris.

'I got here first!' crowed Luke.

'Not fair – my ankle's always worse first thing in the morning,' muttered Mr Harris, climbing up beside Maggie.

'All the more reason for me to drive, then!' said Luke with a placid smile as he started the engine.

It didn't take long for the three of them to gather up the tarpaulins and rope from the top field. As soon as they were back in the truck, they made their way straight for Pear Tree Cottage.

Maggie's smiling face had become more and more serious the closer they got, and by the time he pulled up in her gateway, he could swear she was on the brink of tears. He wasn't surprised. He probably would be too if this was his home.

This really wasn't good.

So much for all his "think positive" talk the night before. The storm had really done a number on the little place.

Stepping out of the truck, the three of them stood side-by-side-by-side, staring at the mess in front of them. Mr Harris had left McGregor in the truck for the time-being, just in case anything else fell from the roof while they were investigating the damage... not that there was much left to come down!

Only one of the several tarpaulins remained in place – dangling limply from one frayed bit of rope. The rest lay scattered around the garden and surrounding fields. Peering around, Luke spotted one flapping on a strand of barbed wire in the distance.

'There's one over there on top of the car too,' said Maggie in a small voice.

Luke nodded. 'Stay there a sec, you two.'

He didn't like pulling rank, but there was no way he wanted either of them to be clonked on the head if there were any more loose slates waiting to fall. Grabbing a bit of wood that had been propping up one of the pieces of hardboard that was now lying prone in the tufty grass, he edged towards the front door. Standing as far back as he could get, he used it to prod the damaged roof – ready to leap out of the way if anything came slipping down.

Nothing shifted. It looked like the storm had finished the job.

He made his way over to Maggie's car and peered at it before shifting a couple of the fallen stones so that he could move the tarp out of the way.

'Good news,' he said, turning to look at the other two, who hadn't budged an inch.

'Seriously?' said Maggie. 'Because now's not the time for jokes.'

'Seriously - I promise,' Luke smiled. 'None of the car windows have been broken. You'll have a few extra dents – but other than cosmetic damage, I think it'll be okay once we've shifted all the stone.'

'Well… that's definitely something!' said Maggie. She smiled at him, but it was clearly costing her quite a bit of effort and it slipped right back of her face again the minute her eyes roamed back to the cottage.

'Might take a while to get it out safely, though,' said Mr Harris, still staring at the car.

Luke nodded, not taking his eyes off Maggie. She was staring as though mesmerised by the sight of the exposed roof beams. The entire place was still dripping with water, and Luke had a nasty feeling it'd be doing that inside, too.

'Do you… do want to have a look inside?' said Luke.

'Do you think it's safe?' said Maggie.

'No,' said Luke sadly. 'We'll have to go careful… but

it might be a good idea for you to see what you're up against. I'm guessing you didn't lock it?'

Maggie shook her head.

Luke wasn't surprised. No one ever locked their homes on Crumcarey. There just wasn't any need.

'Want me to do the honours?' he prompted when Maggie didn't budge.

She just nodded, looking wide-eyed. Luke watched for a moment as Mr Harris put a gentle hand on her shoulder. Good. It's exactly what he wanted to do… but right now, he was more use taking charge of the practical side of things.

Reaching for the doorknob, he pushed the door open and paused. There was no resulting crash… which had to be a good start. Still, he was having a hard time not swearing out loud at the sight that greeted his eyes.

Even though the storm damage was fairly bad inside the hallway, it wasn't the missing roof or the fact that the entire place was alive with the sound of dripping water that had shocked him.

How had Maggie managed to live here so long in this state?!

Russell's attempts at "modernising" were apparent everywhere he looked. Half-stripped walls and chunks of plasterboard with holes bashed in them were the least of his worries, though. It was the exposed electrical wiring and dangling dead ends everywhere that had him on high alert! The first thing they needed to do was to turn the power off... that's if it hadn't already tripped.

'Do you know where the fuse board is?' he said, as Maggie and Mr Harris appeared behind him.

'Of course,' she said in a quiet voice. 'We're old friends.'

'Good,' said Luke. 'Let's get the power turned off – just until we know what the water's got into. We'll have to get someone over to make sure it's all safe.'

Maggie just nodded and pointed to the far end of the hallway. Sure enough, there was an ancient-looking fuse box sitting high on the shadowy wall. There was no way Luke was touching anything inside *that* with his bare hands – even if it should theoretically be safe.

'Back in two secs.'

Dashing back outside, he grabbed the long piece of wood he'd been using to prod at the roof.

'Got the torch with you?' he said, hurrying back to the fuse box.

Maggie nodded. Grabbing it from her pocket, she flicked it on and angled the beam so that he could see what he was doing.

'Perfect,' said Luke, gingerly lifting the cover off the board. Then he let out a sigh of relief. Every single trip switch in there had already flipped over to the *off* position. 'We're good,' he said. 'For now, at least.'

Maggie nodded and then turned to lead the way through to the living room without saying a word.

Luke followed, only to find her standing stock-still,

staring at a scene of devastation. The room was completely open to the elements. He glanced up at the sky through the bare bones of the roof beams and sighed.

Mr Harris let out a breath just behind him, and Luke turned and caught his eye. His uncle simply shrugged – though the look in his eyes clearly conveyed his own horror at the state of the place.

'Well...' said Luke, wanting to break the silence. Then he paused. He needed to choose his words carefully... he wanted to be as tactful as possible. After all, he didn't want to be too negative about the place. Maggie had clearly worked her behind off just to keep it from crumbling. This was her home... even if it could barely be classed as a building right now! 'There's definitely a lot to do... but the walls will be nice and solid. These old stone places were built to last.'

'Yeah... three hundred years ago,' said Maggie in a small voice. 'Maybe we're coming to the end...?'

'Don't be soft, lass!' said Mr Harris in a firm voice. 'This place will be here when your children's children's children are having children.'

Maggie cracked a smile at that, and Luke sent a grateful wink in his uncle's direction.

'He's right, Mags.'

'I'm always right,' said Mr Harris with a nod. 'It looks bad with all the rainwater dripping in, but once we've got some covers back on the roof and everything's dried out a bit, it'll be fine. You'll see.'

A FRESH START ON CRUMCAREY

'Is there anything you want to grab and bring with you?' said Luke.

'With me?' said Maggie, sounding dazed.

'To The Tallyaff,' he said. 'Isn't Olive expecting you for work?'

Maggie blinked up at him in confusion for a moment, and Luke had to forcibly stop himself from reaching out and brushing a long strand of dark hair off her face.

'Shit. Work!' she said, seemingly coming to. 'Gimmie a sec!'

'We'll wait for you outside,' said Luke, suddenly aware that she might need a bit of privacy.

The place might be a dripping mess of half-done jobs, but it was still her home. Now that he knew she wasn't about to get an electric shock, and no slates were teetering in the rafters like the sword of Damocles, he was happy that she was safe.

'I can't believe it,' muttered Mr Harris in a low tone the minute the pair of them stepped back out into the daylight.

'A bit of clearing up to do,' agreed Luke. 'The slates need shifting, and there's probably some woodwork to do before anything else can happen,' he added, nodding at the roof. 'I'm not sure there's any point using tarps again, though… maybe we can find something better to get her through the winter.'

'I wasn't talking about the storm damage!' said Mr Harris, glancing over his shoulder to make sure that

Maggie was still well out of earshot. 'The state that poor girl's been living in!'

'Looks to me like she's done loads,' said Luke. He knew he sounded defensive, but he couldn't help it. He was impressed she'd managed to do as much as she had.

'Aye – I'm not disputing that, lad,' said Mr Harris. 'But there are jobs here no one could manage on their own… not even you!'

Luke nodded and opened his mouth to reply when Maggie appeared in the doorway, hugging a plastic box close to her chest. He raised his eyebrows. He'd been expecting clothes, maybe even some keepsakes she wanted to save from the water… but this was barely big enough to hold more than a notebook or two.

'What have you got in there?'

CHAPTER 13

MAGGIE

Maggie considered changing her clothes. The outfit she was wearing was still decidedly stiff from being baked in front of Luke's wood burner. She kept most of her clothes in plastic boxes, so they *should* be okay... but... she really didn't fancy stripping only to get dripped on. Right now, it felt like it was still raining inside the cottage, and *everything* was soggy.

Maggie quickly decided against it – especially considering Luke and Mr Harris were waiting for her just outside. Worst case scenario, she could beg Olive for the loan of a guest robe while she popped her outfit through the quick wash in The Tallyaff's laundry!

As for grabbing anything else... she was too overwhelmed by the state of her home to think straight. Besides, she didn't have anywhere to stash her stuff, anyway. The car might be miraculously in one piece, but it was still buried under a bunch of roof slates!

In the end, Maggie grabbed just one thing before making her way back outside.

'What have you got in there?' said Luke, curiously eyeballing the plastic box she had clutched to her chest.

'It's the drawings I made of the cottage when we first moved here,' she said, smiling at him.

'Seriously?' said Luke, looking intrigued.

Maggie nodded. She felt slightly nervous. These drawings had stayed hidden away in this plastic box for a very long time. Ever since she'd shown them to Russell, and he'd promptly got the hump. He'd stomped around for hours and then told her that it would be better if she kept her nose out of things. He didn't need the help of a *failed designer*. He wanted Pear Tree Cottage to evolve organically under his care and attention… because he knew best.

'Can we take a look?' said Mr Harris eagerly.

'Oh!' said Maggie in surprise. 'Well… sure, why not.'

She rested the box on the bonnet of the truck and carefully lifted out the wad of drawings, handing them to Mr Harris.

The old man started to look at them one by one, handing them off to Luke as he went.

'Blimey Mags!' he gasped.

'You did these?' said Mr Harris.

'Yeah,' she said.

'What did you say you did at uni?' said Luke.

'Design,' said Maggie quietly. 'I didn't graduate, though.'

'And after that?' said Luke.

'I worked in an architect's office,' she mumbled.

'That explains it,' said Mr Harris, looking impressed.

'Not really,' said Maggie, shifting her weight uncomfortably.

'Why not?' said Luke, shooting her a curious glance.

'Because I was the office cleaner,' she said with a small smile.

'Well,' said Mr Harris, 'I'd say they missed a trick, there!'

Maggie felt her treacherous cheeks turn pink under the implied praise. She wasn't used to it... but she had to admit, it was nice to have someone look through her drawings without turning their noses up at them!

'I know they're not exactly practical,' she said.

'Oh... I don't know...' said Luke slowly. 'Looks like you plan on making the most of what's already available on the island, rather than having to get tons of expensive materials delivered from down south?'

Maggie nodded.

'Good thinking,' murmured Mr Harris, handing another sketch to Luke.

Maggie shifted her weight again, suddenly uncomfortable with the praise. She was ready to get going. She needed to get away from everything to do with the cottage for a while and lose herself in some hard work!

McGregor clearly agreed with her as he gave an impatient *woof* from inside the truck. The poor lad was clearly not used to being held captive while the others had all the fun.

'I like them,' said Luke, completely ignoring McGregor's less-than-subtle hints. 'It's like… now I can see *why* you want to live here.'

'I… erm… thank you,' said Maggie. 'First things first, I guess – I need to get those tarpaulins back on the roof.' She felt her shoulders sag at the thought of the amount of work that lay ahead of her just to make the cottage inhabitable again.

'Not slates?' said Mr Harris.

'You know, right now I don't really care what goes up there!' she shrugged, giving him a small smile. 'If I can figure out how to get a roof up there that keeps the weather out before the winter arrives, I'll be thrilled.' She paused and let out a huge sigh. 'I'll figure it out. Somehow.'

'Of course you will,' said Luke stoutly.

'Look, I'm really sorry to be a pain,' she said, 'but I think I'd better head over to The Tallyaff before Olive sends out a search party!'

Luke glanced at his watch and swore.

'Shit, you're right – sorry Maggie,' he said, carefully laying her drawings back inside the box. 'Connor's going to be wondering where on earth I am, too!'

'Drop us both off on your way, lad,' said Mr Harris. 'I could do with a coffee and some breakfast after all the excitement. You can take the truck - I'm sure I can grab a lift back from someone.'

∽

'Thanks for the ride… and the rescue… and everything!' said Maggie, scrambling down from the truck and shifting out of the way as McGregor made his own break for freedom.

It had been a weird drive. Mr Harris had spent the entire journey complaining about the non-existent traffic, and Luke had just nodded along, sending her sidelong glances that kept making her want to giggle despite the fact that she'd just left her home in tatters behind her.

'No worries, Mags,' said Luke with a grin. 'Catch up very soon, okay?'

'I'd like that,' she said quietly.

'Oh… would you mind if I keep your drawings for a bit and have another look through them?' he said, already putting the truck in gear.

'Yeah, of course!' said Maggie in surprise.

'See ya!'

Maggie stared at the truck as it pulled away from her, feeling strangely bereft.

'Idiot,' she muttered.

'What's that?'

She jumped and turned to find Mr Harris waiting for her patiently.

'Oh, nothing,' she said with a little shake of her head.

'Come on, lass. You've had a bit of a morning of it,' he said.

'I guess…'

'Nothing a bit of hard work won't cure,' he added with a grin, opening the door of The Tallyaff for her. 'I need that coffee!'

Maggie smiled at him and led the way inside.

'Maggie lovely!' said Olive, dashing towards her from behind the bar. 'Are you okay?'

'I'm so sorry,' said Maggie. She was a good twenty minutes late for her shift. 'I should have called!'

'Don't be daft,' said Olive shaking her head. 'I was just worried. I literally just got off the phone with Stella – she said she drove past your cottage just now, and you've lost most of your roof!'

Maggie nodded.

'You're not hurt?' demanded Olive, grabbing her hands and looking her up and down, searching for injuries.

'She was at Luke's,' said Mr Harris blandly, plonking himself down on his usual bar stool and throwing dirty looks around at the visitors who must have arrived on the early morning ferry.

'Luke's?' echoed Olive, her eyes lighting up with the promise of impending gossip.

'Yep. Caught her there myself,' said Mr Harris. 'In her *underpants!*'

Olive's jaw dropped dramatically, and Maggie started to laugh.

'Want the really filthy bit of gossip?' she said.

'Um – YES!' said Olive going wide-eyed in anticipation.

'They weren't even *my* underpants… they were Luke's!'

The pronouncement drew a gasp from both Olive *and* Mr Harris… and then the pair of them dissolved into a fit of giggles.

Maggie caught the eye of a decidedly surprised-looking tourist who was waiting patiently at the bar to place an order. She smiled at the woman.

'Don't mind them,' she said. 'They've had a bit of a strange morning. How can I help?'

From that moment on, Maggie's day didn't let up. After serving Mr Harris, she'd filled Olive in on the details of what had happened the previous evening between serving late breakfasts to The Tallyaff's guests. Then, she manned the bar while Olive changed over the vacant rooms in time for their new arrivals.

Maggie was just waving Mr Harris off when all the passengers from the morning plane turned up. To say she was run off her feet was an understatement, but it was exactly what she needed. She was so busy that she was able to completely forget about the disaster zone that was waiting for her back at the cottage.

Until home time, that was.

'Erm… Olive… I don't suppose either of the hire cars are free?' she said, wiping down the bar for what felt like the millionth time that day.

Maggie could kick herself that she hadn't even considered this problem until now. Not only had she not given a thought to how she was meant to survive in a cottage with no electricity and very little roof, but she also hadn't considered how she was going to get back there without her car.

'Nope, sorry love,' said Olive. 'They're both out with visitors.'

'Oh. Of course they are,' she sighed. 'And… do we have any empty rooms?'

Maggie didn't even know why she was bothering to ask. She already *knew* the answer to that. No. The Tallyaff was full to the brim for the foreseeable.

Olive shook her head again.

'Maybe there's something available over at the conference centre,' said Maggie.

'Oh no you don't!' said Olive. 'You'll stay in my spare room before you end up over there. They've only got one decent room, and from what I've heard Joyce has commandeered it.'

'Well… thanks!' said Maggie, smiling at Olive. 'I might have to take you up on that offer, you know?'

'You're welcome any time,' said Olive. 'But no need to make any plans straight away. Maybe… take a look at your place with fresh eyes this evening and see what's what. You were still in shock this morning.'

Maggie bit her lip and nodded. Somehow, she didn't think "fresh eyes" were going to do her any favours. And even if things did miraculously look better... she didn't have a car to get there.

'Head off, lovely. You've had a busy day,' said Olive. 'There's someone waiting for you out in the carpark.'

'There is?!' said Maggie in surprise. For one horrible moment, her mind flew to the possibility that Russell might have suddenly reappeared. It would be typical of him to turn up just as she hit rock bottom.

Just when she'd met someone who made her toes tingle every time she thought about him.

Wait... maybe it was Luke outside?!

'Thanks Olive!' said Maggie, brightening up considerably at the thought. Suddenly she couldn't wait to get out into the carpark. 'See you tomorrow. I promise not to be late!'

Maggie practically jogged out of The Tallyaff and into the car park. Sure enough, Mr Harris's old truck was sitting there waiting for her... but it wasn't Luke behind the wheel.

'Mr Harris?' she said, opening the door. 'You came back for me!'

'Can't leave you stranded at work now, can I?' chuckled the old man. 'Hop in. Give McGregor a shove – he likes to take up the entire seat.'

It didn't take long for the little dog to climb into her lap and fall asleep.

'Good day?' said Mr Harris.

'Not bad,' said Maggie with a smile. 'I mean... all things considered. It was super busy.'

'That's what I keep saying,' said Mr Harris. 'You're busy. Roads are busy. There are people everywhere!'

Maggie grinned, wishing Luke was sitting next to her so that they could share a conspiratorial eye roll.

'So... you got the truck back from Luke, then?' she said.

'Aye,' said Mr Harris, shifting slightly in his seat. 'He finished a bit earlier than expected and I had some things I needed to collect from here and there. Thought I'd pick you up at the same time.'

'Well... thank you!' said Maggie, glancing out of the window at the wing mirror. Sure enough, she could just make out a pile of *something* in the back of the truck, covered over in what looked very much like one of her errant tarpaulins.

Well, she certainly didn't mind if Mr Harris needed to commandeer them - especially considering they'd blown into his field! Besides, after everything he and Luke had already done for her, she owed them both – big time!

Maggie leaned back and did her best to relax. The window was open a crack, and the fresh air was making McGregor's ears flap around. She smiled, stroking his head. She was getting decidedly fond of this little dog!

'Right… so… nearly at your place!' said Mr Harris.

Maggie raised her eyebrows. She couldn't put her finger on why, but that announcement had been a bit… odd.

Leaning forward in her seat, she peered along the road, half-dreading the first sight of her poor, battered cottage.

'What on earth?!' she gasped.

It… had a roof. Or… *nearly* a whole roof, anyway.

It looked quite strange. She was so used to seeing it covered over with green tarps that it almost felt like they were pulling up at the wrong house.

Mr Harris drew the truck to a standstill and grinned across at her. She stared back at him, her mouth gaping in shock. Then she turned back to the cottage again. The grass on the driveway was marked with dozens of tyre tracks. There had clearly been a lot of action here today!

'What… what's going on?'

CHAPTER 14

LUKE

*L*uke only just managed to clamber down off the ladder in time.

Phew!

He crouched in the grass at the side of the cottage and peered at Maggie's face through the windscreen of the truck. He didn't have a completely clear view, but it was pretty obvious that she was confused… and shocked… and surprised.

Luke's stomach flipped. Had they done the right thing? He desperately wanted this to be a *good* surprise!

'Luke Harris!' demanded Maggie, flinging open the door of the truck and peering around in search of him. 'I know you're here – come out this instant!'

Luke straightened up, grinning from ear to ear. He caught sight of his uncle's laughing face and shook his head. That man couldn't keep a secret for two seconds!

'Okay, okay... I've got an apology to make,' he said giving McGregor a pat before striding towards Maggie.

'An apology?' she said. 'I... you... but why?' She rubbed her face. 'Am I hallucinating right now, or does my cottage have a new roof?'

'Well... kind of,' said Luke.

'Kind of?' she said, shaking her head. 'That's a roof, Luke. A *roof!*'

'That's what I wanted to apologise for,' he muttered. 'I *was* just going to put the tarps back... but I was talking to Connor about it, and he knew someone who had a whole stack of these black metal sheets. I knew they'd be easier than the tarps... and they'll stay put better too and do a better job and—'

'I can't believe you did all this!' she said, running her fingers through her hair.

Luke watched her for a long moment, waiting for her to say something else. He still couldn't tell if she was pleased or not. It *had* been a big gamble to go ahead without checking she was cool with it first...

'Connor helped me to collect it and unload it,' said Luke quietly. 'He helped me get it in place too.'

'I can't believe it,' said Maggie, shaking her head slightly, as though the new roof might disappear if she kept doing it. 'Can you tell me where you got it? I'll do my best to pay them back as soon as I can.'

'Oh!' said Luke, suddenly understanding why she was looking worried rather than relieved. 'You don't need to worry about that - they were glad to get rid of it!'

'Seriously?' she said, and Luke could swear he could see the weight start to lift from her shoulders.

'Yep,' he said with a smile. 'They said you were welcome to it. I'm not quite finished yet, but it's nearly there.'

'I can't believe it!' she said again, staring at her new roof, this time with far more enthusiasm.

'I'm afraid I haven't managed to get the windows fixed yet though,' said Luke.

'I didn't realise they'd been broken!' she said.

'Not... not last night,' said Luke carefully. 'But you had a few panes missing?'

Maggie nodded.

'Well, someone on Little Crum had some really nice ones they were going to use to build a greenhouse. They're going to bring them over by boat tomorrow.' He grinned at her.

Maggie looked like someone had just clonked her on the head with a baseball bat.

'What about their greenhouse?' she said faintly.

'Well, it never really happened,' said Luke with a shrug. 'They've had the windows wrapped up in their barn for a decade, so they're quite keen to get them out of the way. Anyway... I *am* sorry.'

'I don't get why you keep apologising?!' said Maggie with a bubble of laughter.

'It's... it's not exactly like your drawings,' he said. 'I

know you had slate tiles… and the windows that are coming aren't quite the same shape you drew in.'

'But they're windows instead of bits of board?' she said.

'Well… yes?' said Luke.

'Are you sure I didn't die in the storm last night?' she laughed. 'Is this… am I in heaven?'

Luke chuckled as Maggie shook her head again.

'Alright you two, I'm joining in the fun now!' said Mr Harris, hopping down from the truck. 'What do you think then, Mags?'

'It's amazing,' said Maggie. 'Thank you, Luke!'

'Joint effort,' said Luke quickly. 'Uncle Harris has spent all day zooming around the island, collecting bits and pieces we needed to… erm… to do the job.' He winced. He'd nearly given the next bit of the surprise away!

'Thank you!' said Maggie, turning to the old man and wrapping him in a hug.

'You're a good lass!' he said delightedly. 'Even if you did start the day wearing Luke's underpants.'

'Ohhh…' said Luke pulling a face. 'I think you ought to know he's been telling that story all day!'

Maggie grinned at Mr Harris as she pulled back. 'Me too!' she laughed.

Luke rolled his eyes and tutted. 'Two peas in a pod.'

Mr Harris's entire face crumpled in delight.

'I've had the best day,' he said. 'Had a chance to chat

with people I haven't seen for ages. Perfect excuse to nip in and natter over a coffee.'

'Everyone's been keen to get involved,' said Luke. 'I… I hope you don't mind. They all just wanted to help you out.'

'Of course I don't mind,' said Maggie, looking blown away. 'I… can't believe it. That all the locals would want to help someone like me.'

'What do you mean, daft girl?' said Mr Harris, patting her shoulder. '*Someone like you* - honestly. Don't you realise… you *are* one of the locals.'

Luke watched as Maggie had to blink away tears. It was as much as he could do to stop himself from going over there and scooping her up in a great big hug… but she was already overwhelmed, and there was still more to show her!

'Why don't you take the lass inside and show her what's been going on in there too?' said Mr Harris gently. 'I'll stay out here and give McGregor a chance to stretch his legs. He's been in the truck with me most of the day!'

'Wait… there's more?' gasped Maggie.

Luke nodded.

'Go with him and see!' twinkled Mr Harris.

'After you?' said Luke.

'Oh… okay…' said Maggie.

Luke followed her as she picked her way towards the front door. They made slow progress as she kept pausing to peer up at the roof.

'Erm… where are we heading?' she said, stepping through the front door at last. 'Wait… the wiring!'

'That was Connor,' said Luke. 'He's been here most of the day too. Decided to take the day off when he heard what happened last night. He's great with electrics, so he's undone all the—'

Luke paused. He didn't want to use the words "death trap" or "disaster waiting to happen" in front of Maggie, no matter how much they'd been bandied around during the day.

'—he's dealt with the issues,' he amended.

There. That sounded less horrific!

'I can't believe it!' she said.

'Head through to the main room,' he said.

Maggie did so, coming to an abrupt halt just inside the door. Luke wasn't that surprised – it did look a *lot* better in there.

'How… *how?!*' gasped Maggie.

All the water had been mopped up, anything cloth that could be removed had been taken away, run through multiple tumble dryers around the island, and then returned.

Two large dehumidifiers had appeared from opposite ends of the island – their owners keen to help out in any way they could. They stood in the middle of the room, rumbling away and sucking moisture out of the air for all they were worth.

'It's mostly Ivy's work in here,' said Luke. 'She

A FRESH START ON CRUMCAREY

scrubbed, wiped, dried, stripped… and basically just tried to sort out anything the water got to.'

'I can't believe she did all that for me,' said Maggie.

'Heads up – there was one major casualty from this whole thing,' said Luke.

'Uh oh,' said Maggie. 'Go on… I can take it…'

'Your couch,' said Luke. 'We're doing our best to dry it out, but a slate fell right onto it and the weight has damaged one of the arms. I think it's a goner, I'm afraid.'

Maggie shrugged. 'If that's the only real damage in here, then I got off lightly.'

Luke nodded. He had to agree… it could have been so much worse. He wasn't going to say it out loud, but the image of Maggie sitting on that sofa when the slate fell had been haunting him all day!

'Just as well you don't have fitted carpet,' said Luke, 'means it'll air out a lot quicker in here. Your rug is still drip-drying in one of Uncle Harris's barns.'

'We *have* done a call out for some carpet for you, though,' said Mr Harris, pottering in to join them.

'You have?' said Maggie in surprise, turning to look at him.

'Of course! In fact, I've got it in the back of the truck.'

'Already?' said Luke, raising his eyebrows. 'I thought that wasn't coming until tomorrow!'

'I got a call on my way over to collect our girl here, so I took a detour,' said Mr Harris with a shrug. 'Just as well I had the tarp still in the truck, otherwise the cat would have been out of the bag.'

'I can't believe it!' gasped Maggie, her hands flying to her face.

'Now, don't go getting all excited,' warned Mr Harris with a little frown. 'I'm not exactly thrilled with the weird patterns – some people have seriously weird taste in my opinion. Even so, it'll warm it up a bit in here for you, and you can always hide it with a few more rugs.'

'Amazing!' said Maggie.

'Seriously, Mags,' said Luke. 'I'd withhold judgment until you've seen it. 1970s swirls were all the rage up here on Crumcarey.'

'Aye, true that,' nodded Mr Harris. 'Come take a peep at it. I've got all sorts of other bits and bobs in there too… more stuff than I can remember.'

'What do you mean?' said Maggie.

'Let's go have a look!' said Luke.

The three of them traipsed out of a very different little cottage than they'd left that morning. Mr Harris made a beeline for the back of the truck and flipped the edge of the tarp back.

'Oh, wow!' chuckled Maggie, staring at the carpet.

'I did warn you,' said Mr Harris.

'I quite like it,' said Luke, cocking his head.

'Yeah… me too,' said Maggie. 'It's got a bit of a cool retro vibe going on.'

'Well, I think you both need your heads checking,'

A FRESH START ON CRUMCAREY

said Mr Harris, 'but I'm glad you're happy. And there's an armchair, a bureau desk thingy...'

'All sorts!' gasped Maggie.

'You don't have to take it all,' said Luke quickly, 'not if you don't want it.'

'Aye, that's true too,' said Mr Harris. 'You can choose what you want, and I'll stash the rest in one of the barns at the farm... it'll find other homes in no time.'

'Thank you... both... so much,' said Maggie.

Luke noticed she was blinking hard as she turned and kissed Mr Harris on the cheek. Then she turned to him and flung her arms around his neck, kissing him firmly – warmly - on the cheek too.

'It's our pleasure,' said Luke.

'Aye,' agreed his uncle. 'It's what we do on Crumcarey. We look after our own.'

Luke felt the moment Maggie burst into tears – mainly because she buried her damp face in his neck and sobbed right into his jumper.

Somehow, he didn't mind in the slightest.

CHAPTER 15

MAGGIE

'All right, you two, break it up, break it up!' grumbled Mr Harris from somewhere behind them.

It was enough to bring a watery grin to Maggie's face, and she reluctantly stepped out of Luke's comforting hug.

Feeling a bit sheepish, she swiped the tears from the corner of her eyes with her sleeve. It was hard not to feel like a rabbit caught in the headlights – there was so much to take in. Her little cottage had been transformed.

Sure, the walls were still green here and there, and the spiders were still very much in evidence in the corners – at least where they hadn't been blown away by the storm – but now she had a roof that she wasn't going to have to check on every single evening. She had electrics that weren't a health hazard. And it was all thanks to Luke and Mr Harris and this amazing community that seemed to be intent on claiming her as one of its own.

This was no longer the house that she and Russell had bought without even viewing it. It was no longer the house that Russell had slowly eroded into a death trap.

This was now... it felt like it could be... home.

'You look like you're about to cry again,' said Luke, looking half-amused, half-fearful.

Maggie punched him playfully on the arm and shook her head. 'Happy tears. Really happy.'

'Good.'

'Aye!' agreed Mr Harris. 'Now, stop your lollygagging the pair of you. No time for standing around – we've got carpet to unload... and a whole load of other random stuff for Maggie to give the thumbs up or thumbs down to!'

If anyone had asked Maggie when she'd left her shift at The Tallyaff whether she'd have the energy in her to spend an hour unloading heavy rolls of carpet and furniture, she might have simply curled up and burst into tears. And not the happy kind! Instead... here she was, having the time of her life!

There were far more treasures hiding in the back of Mr Harris's truck than she'd realised. She couldn't believe how generous everyone had been... and she had no idea how she was going to pay them all back.

'You mustn't think of it like that,' said Luke, shaking his head. 'It doesn't work like that up here.'

'True,' said Mr Harris, who was standing back and directing proceedings. He'd been doing a lot of that. Right now, he was overseeing them manoeuvring a particularly heavy oak kitchen table through the front door. 'People just want to help out where they can. They were glad to see the back of most of this stuff. Not because it's rubbish, but because it's hard to get rid of things you're finished with when you live on an island!'

Maggie couldn't help but nod as the reality of that logic sunk in. It was a small community – people either wanted your stuff... or they didn't. There weren't really many other options after that – other than stashing things away in increasingly packed outbuildings.

Even so, she felt like she'd been given a pot of gold with all these gifts. There was furniture, kitchen equipment – and there was even a back boiler for her wood burner turning up in the morning.

'It'll give you hot running water!' said Luke. 'Someone bought it for their own stove, but they were sent the wrong size and the supplier didn't want it back!'

'But... that's amazing,' said Maggie, shaking her head. 'I'll need to find someone to plumb it in, though.'

'It'll be done before you even get back from work,' chuckled Luke. Then his face became serious. 'If... if you want it to be, of course.'

'Of course!' said Maggie. 'I mean… yes please! I have no idea how I'll ever re-pay you both, I—'

'Enough of all that, lass,' said Mr Harris gently. 'There'll be a time when someone needs something you can offer, and you won't even think twice about it. It's the way it works. Always has, always will.'

Maggie thought about arguing again, and then simply nodded. It was starting to sink in. She was a member of this community – and this was a part of what that meant.

At long last, the back of Mr Harris's truck was empty and the cottage was decidedly fuller than it had been that morning. It didn't feel cramped, though – just full of possibilities.

'I think it might be time to leave you to it for a bit?' said Luke gently, catching her yawning widely with her backside propped against the edge of her new kitchen table.

'Should I make a list of what's happening tomorrow?' she said, through another howling yawn.

'No need, unless you want to?' said Luke. 'I'll get the back boiler hooked up, and we'll go from there?'

'Thank you – both of you – for the best surprise!' she said.

'Grand lass, see you tomorrow for morning coffee?' said Mr Harris. 'I can give you a lift again if you'd like?'

'Oh!' said Maggie, who hadn't even thought about that.

'Your car's fine and good to go,' said Luke. 'Connor checked it over earlier...'

'That's brilliant!' said Maggie, shaking her head as the sense of overwhelm threatened to hit her again.

'I'll be here to pick you up about ten minutes before your shift, then?' said Mr Harris.

'But...' Maggie stopped herself from turning the offer down out of sheer idiotic politeness. 'Thank you – I'd love that.'

'Grand. Right, lad, let's get out of here,' said Mr Harris, and Maggie watched him tug at Luke's sleeve.

'You've forgotten something!' she said with a grin, as she spotted a small heap snuggled up on her discarded jumper.

'What?' said Luke in surprise.

Maggie didn't miss the strange look on his face. Was that... *hope?* She shook her head. She was tired and probably not thinking straight. There was no way he was expecting – or hoping for - a kiss... was there?

She wished!

'McGregor!' she said, her voice coming out in a husky rasp as she pointed at the snoozing dog.

'Well, he's certainly made himself at home!' laughed Mr Harris. 'Luke, will you do the honours?'

Luke nodded, and then with a small smile in Maggie's direction, he scooped the little dog up in his arms.

Maggie stepped towards the pair of them and stroked McGregor's silky ears.

'Thanks for all your help,' she said.

'It's no problem,' said Luke.

'I was talking to McGregor,' said Maggie, giving Luke a little wink. Then she dropped a kiss onto the still-sleeping dog's head.

∾

The cottage felt strangely quiet as Mr Harris's truck pulled away, even with the rattling drone of the two dehumidifiers doing their thing to remove the last traces of the internal rainstorm.

Letting out a long, happy sigh, Maggie turned on the spot, surveying the scene properly. She couldn't believe how much work everyone had done to make sure she could stay in her home.

It would take a while to get all her new bits and pieces set out just the way she wanted them – but Maggie felt like the cottage was breathing a sigh of relief under its new metal roof.

It was loved. It was being looked after.

'Time to do the same thing for yourself!' Maggie yawned. She was going to get changed and make herself something for tea – and then she was going to fall onto her mattress and pass out!

Heading through to her bedroom – the one space she hadn't even entered yet as it was the one room that hadn't seen any storm damage - Maggie came to an abrupt halt.

'Oh my goodness!' she gasped.

Her mattress was no longer lying directly on the cold, damp flagstones. It was sitting on a rugged-looking bed base made out of huge pieces of timber that were held together with giant bolts.

On top of her beautifully smooth duvet and plumped pillows, there was a scrap of paper. With shaking fingers, Maggie reached out and unfolded it.

It's nothing special – just bits of the old cow shed roof. Uncle Harris helped. Hope you like it! Luke x

Maggie ran a fingertip over the kiss at the end of the note. There was just one of them, and it was only small – but she couldn't help the warm, wide smile that spread over her face.

This should have been one of the hardest days of her life. Instead, it had turned into one of the best… and she had a feeling she was in for plenty more just like it.

CHAPTER 16

LUKE

Luke was having the time of his life. He had tons to do – and that was just the way he liked it.

Putting his foot down, he urged Connor's truck to speed up a bit as he pressed the button to turn on the radio. His friend had been more than happy to let Luke commandeer his truck for the day – which was a bit of a blessing, considering Mr Harris had cows to tend to after he'd taken Maggie to work. Luke knew his uncle no longer checked on his beasts on foot – he preferred to do it in style - trundling around the fields in his truck.

Luke hummed a couple of lines of a country tune as it blared from the radio, and McGregor promptly started to howl from the passenger seat.

'Nice harmonies there, lad!' chuckled Luke, glancing in his rear-view mirror just to make sure the windows and back boiler he'd collected were still safe and sound in the back. He was glad of the little dog's company today – it would be a bit quiet in Maggie's little cottage otherwise, considering it had a hive of activity of the previous day as everyone had pulled together for the main part of the clean-up operation.

'What do you say to a quick detour first?' said Luke, glancing down at the little dog.

McGregor let out a little woof and wagged his wiry tail.

'Ice cream, you say? Okay – sounds like a plan.'

Luke indicated and pulled off the road into the little patch of parking above Big Sandy. He hadn't been expecting to have to squeeze into a spot between one of Olive's hire cars and a very snazzy-looking camper van, complete with a couple of surfboards strapped to the roof.

Hopping out, he quickly clipped McGregor's rarely-used lead onto his collar – just in case the feisty little fellow decided to make "friends" with the tourists. Then he grabbed the box containing Maggie's drawings. He wanted to take another look at them while he had this rare moment to himself.

'Ready?' he said, glancing down at McGregor, who was already straining towards the beach.

Luke grinned and ambled towards Ruby, the gorgeous vintage ice cream van that belonged to Stella and Frank.

'Huh… a queue!' murmured Luke, spotting five or

six people lined up, waiting their turn at the hatch. It was a bit of a rare sight on Crumcarey… in fact, it was unheard of. Part of him wished he'd thought to bring his phone so that he could snap a photo to commemorate the occasion!

Joining the back of the line and keeping McGregor on a very short leash as he strained to sniff at the nearest pair of ankles, Luke craned his neck, trying to catch Stella's eye. It took a couple of seconds, but when she did look up, Stella shot him a bemused grin – and then shrugged. Clearly, she was as surprised by the sudden rush as he was.

Crumcarey was alive with visitors – and going by the excited chatter of the ice cream hunters ahead of him, they all seemed to be overjoyed to have discovered such an unexpected opportunity to grab a 99 with a flake and real raspberry sauce!

'Excuse me?' said the woman in front, turning to him.

'Sorry!' he said in horror, realising too late that McGregor had hold of the ends of her shoelaces and was tugging at them with all his might.

'Don't worry about him!' chuckled the woman. 'He seems to be having fun…'

Luke smiled uneasily at that. As long as the little monster's fun didn't head towards the slightly more vicious kind! Luke had witnessed a good few ankles being savaged in McGregor's youth, though he did seem to have mellowed a bit in his old age.

'I just wanted to ask,' said the woman, 'you're local, right?'

'Erm…' Luke thought about explaining his complex relationship with the island he'd always thought of as home… and then he shrugged. 'Yep. Local,' he agreed.

'Well, I was just wondering if you could tell me where the art gallery is?'

'Art gallery?' he said raising his eyebrows.

'Yes – one that sells paintings like the ones in this!' she pulled a copy of the new Crumcarey guidebook out of her pocket, and Luke caught a glimpse of one of Rowan's beautiful paintings on the front cover.

'I don't think there's a gallery on Crumcarey,' said Luke.

'Oh,' said the woman, wilting slightly. 'That's a shame, I would have loved to buy an original while we're here. I thought the artist was local.'

'She is – but she's off painting around the world at the moment,' said Luke. 'Why don't you ask Olive at The Tallyaff? If Rowan's got any paintings for sale, she'll know all about it. I'm sure she'll be happy to put you in touch.'

'Oh, perfect,' said the woman. 'Thank you!'

Luke smiled, and then gave McGregor's lead a surreptitious tug, just as the little dog started to nibble at the bottom of the woman's jeans. McGregor gave him a look as if to say *spoilsport.*

It didn't take too long for Stella and Frank to make their way through the queue. As the crowd dispersed,

A FRESH START ON CRUMCAREY

Luke ambled up to the window and Stella greeted him with a broad smile.

'How's it going?' he said.

'Mad,' said Frank, grinning at him from over Stella's shoulder.

'Good,' added Stella.

'Unexpected!' they said together, and then started laughing.

Luke smiled at the pair of them. Stella was Olive's daughter, and she'd moved back to Crumcarey not that long ago, bringing with her both her true loves – Ruby and Frank.

The pair of them were mad about the cold weather and isolation Crumcarey offered, so he could only imagine this unprecedented influx of visitors was a little bit unsettling for them.

'It's all good,' said Stella. 'We're making the most of the visitors now and looking forward to a peaceful winter.'

'Good call,' said Luke. 'On that note… can I have a 99 with a flake please.'

'Fudge sauce?' said Frank. 'I've just made a new batch.'

'Oh yes!' breathed Luke, lifting his nose and catching the hot, sweet caramel scent in the air. Maybe he should bring Maggie down here when she was done with her shift…

'Why don't you grab a seat. I'll bring it over to you,' said Stella.

Luke grinned. There weren't any seats in sight, but he was more than happy to plonk his bum down onto one of the wide, flat stones at the top of the beach while he waited.

Now that the rest of the visitors had disappeared, he decided it would be safe to let McGregor off his lead. The little dog promptly pottered off to do a circuit of the van, licking up patches of spilt ice cream as he went, before ambling down onto the beach to chase bits of seaweed as they fluttered in the fresh sea breeze.

Luke rested Maggie's box of drawings on his lap and took the lid off. Then, carefully taking hold of the bundle of pages, he began to look through them.

They were just as beautiful as he remembered – and even more detailed. So – it hadn't just been his first impression then – Maggie was seriously skilled. As for the materials she'd used, they really were well-considered.

Obviously, this being an island without any trees, new timber wasn't exactly easy to come by. But there *were* plenty of abandoned buildings with roofs that had caved in. That meant there were old rafters and sarking boards that could easily be re-purposed with a bit of extra work. There was any amount of stone available, too - and the thick roof slates from the ancient buildings made beautiful flagstones.

'What have you got there?' said Stella, sinking down next to him on the stone.

'Oh!' said Luke, looking up in surprise. He hadn't heard her approaching. Frank was making his way over from the van too, bearing his 99 complete with a flake and plenty of gooey fudge sauce. 'You guys on a break?' he said, rather than answering her question. Maggie had entrusted her drawings to him... but she hadn't given him permission to show them around.

'A much-needed break!' said Frank, sinking down on the other side of him so that he was sandwiched between them.

'Here,' said Stella, removing the plastic box from his lap and then taking the wad of drawings from him so that he could hold his ice cream.

'Cheers!' said Luke.

Well... it would be rude to try and hide them now, wouldn't it?!

Hopefully, Maggie wouldn't mind. He didn't know her that well yet, but he didn't think she would.

'Wow!' said Stella, glancing down at the top drawing. 'Luke, where did you get these?'

'Maggie,' he said through a thick mouthful of ice cream and sauce.

'The lass at Brae Burn?' said Stella.

'The place they renamed Pear Tree Cottage?' said Frank.

Stella snorted – clearly, she disliked the new name as much as Maggie did. 'Aye, that's her,' said Luke, watching as Stella carefully looked through the drawings, one page at a time, before handing them over to Frank.

Luke winced slightly as the top page picked up a tiny drop of fudge sauce on its way past. Frank quickly whipped out a clean handkerchief and dabbed at it.

Oops, he'd have some explaining to do!

'Sorry!' said Stella. 'Erm… maybe tell her that's her coupon for two free ice creams?'

'I will!' Luke laughed.

'These are really something,' said Frank.

'Right?' agreed Stella. 'I love them. Can you tell her we love them?'

'Erm… sure?' said Luke.

'I mean… I don't really know her, but she's clearly a natural,' said Stella. 'I know she's only just starting to brave the rest of us, and she's had that disaster at her cottage, but do you think she might have time to come and look at our place?'

'Great idea!' said Frank, nodding enthusiastically without taking his eyes off the drawings in his hands. 'Our place isn't anywhere near as bad as Maggie's, but we just don't have any ideas about what to do with it.'

'We like small, cosy spaces,' said Stella, 'like the van. So we don't want to open it up like a few other people have done on the island.'

'Open plan… yuck!' said Frank with an exaggerated shudder.

Stella snorted. 'Yeah, I agree. But there's something about the layout at our place that doesn't really make sense, and we're useless – we can't figure out what needs to change to make it right.'

'And judging by these... Maggie might just have some ideas,' said Frank.

'Well, I can ask her – no harm in that, right?' said Luke.

CHAPTER 17

MAGGIE

Maggie was having another fantastic day at The Tallyaff. She might only be on her third shift, but she'd already reached the point where she couldn't imagine life without her new job. How had she survived so long with so little human contact?

After Luke and Mr Harris's island-wide call for help the previous day, the floodgates had opened. People had been bouncing up to Maggie all morning, offering building supplies and all manner of things to help make Pear Tree Cottage a bit more cosy and weatherproof – plus tea and sympathy whenever she needed it.

As well as being touched to the point she'd teared up several times, Maggie had also spent a great deal of time apologising in advance for the fact that she probably wasn't going to be able to remember everyone's names. She might have prided herself on knowing the faces of the locals before she'd started her new job, but now she knew their names, where they lived, their family history going back at least three generations – and their coffee and pastry preferences too!

She was also discovering that there were dozens of social groups on the island that she'd had no idea about.

'So, you'll come along to the knitting club?' said the elderly lady, leaning heavily on her stick as she beamed at Maggie through her thick glasses. 'It's over at my place next time. We all bring a bit of baking to share and have a grand time.'

'I'll… sure!' said Maggie, finding it completely impossible to say no, even though she didn't have a clue how to knit.

'Don't worry if you don't have the necessaries, I've got plenty to start you off with!'

'Oh, wow,' said Maggie, wondering if her new friend was a mind reader. If only she could remember her name! 'Well, thanks. I might need a lesson in the basics, too.'

'It'll be my pleasure,' she said. 'Mr Harris!' she added, nodding at the old man who was still propping up the bar, nursing his second espresso of the morning.

'Mrs Harcus,' he replied with his own nod.

That was it – Sue Harcus!

Maggie did her best to stifle a giggle as Mr Harris rolled his eyes.

'What was that for?' murmured Maggie in amusement as soon as she was sure the Sue was out of earshot.

'No dogs allowed at the knitting group,' he tutted. 'Not that McGregor really cares. Just a bunch of knots and silly sticks!'

'You missing him, huh?' said Maggie.

'Don't be soft,' said Mr Harris. 'He doesn't get on very well with the cows, so it's for the best.'

'What do you think about the swimming group Anna was telling me about earlier?' she said. She'd been invited to that too. In fact, she'd been invited to enough groups and events to fill up every day of the week for the rest of the year if she agreed to go to all of them.

'Sharks,' said Mr Harris, shaking his head. 'And jellyfish.'

'I thought you liked swimming with Anna?' said Maggie in surprise.

'I do,' nodded Mr Harris. 'But I have private sessions in the pool up at Crum House. It's nice and warm in there... no sharks. You should look into it!'

'Okay,' said Maggie, nodding. 'I will.'

'Blimey girl, you're a popular one this morning,' said Olive, bustling over to her with a broad smile on her face.

'Sorry!' said Maggie automatically. 'I didn't mean to spend so much time gossiping!'

'Get on with you,' tutted Olive with a good-natured eyeroll. 'It's been brilliant. I think half the island has rocked up to see you this morning – and most of them stopped for a cuppa and something to eat. We're almost out of pastries!'

Maggie breathed a sigh of relief. At least her socialising had been good for business.

'Oh,' said Olive, 'I meant to say – I've got some half-priced diaries out the back… just in case you need to write down all these invitations you've been getting!'

'Have you got a social secretary lurking out there too that I can borrow?' Maggie laughed.

'Not quite!' said Olive with a grin. 'I've got some stickers you could use for the important dates, though?'

'Actually, that'd be great,' said Maggie.

'Only dragons or unicorns left,' said Olive.

'Dragons sound perfect!'

'Should be sharks,' muttered Mr Harris as Olive disappeared to fetch them.

'Hey,' said Maggie, turning to Mr Harris, 'now that it's a bit quieter, I wanted to say thank you. Properly, I mean.'

Mr Harris instantly started to shake his head, but Maggie reached out and laid her hand on top of his weathered, gnarly one.

'Seriously,' she said. 'Thank you. For everything you've done – driving me around, being my friend… and for everything at the cottage.'

'That was mostly Luke,' said Mr Harris gruffly, taking a sip of espresso with his free hand.

'Yes, Luke's been brilliant too,' said Maggie, deciding to let him off the hook as he clearly didn't know what to do with her gratitude.

'Aye, he's a good lad,' said Mr Harris. 'He just gets bored quickly. It's always been his problem. He finds it hard to settle to anything or anywhere for very long.'

'I guess that's why he's good at so many things,' said Maggie.

'Yes, he is that,' said Mr Harris. 'He's worked all over the place, but I don't mind telling you that I'd love to see him settle down here on Crumcarey. He's only really here to help with the ferry and the dive school boat... and I know as soon as that work's done, he'll disappear off somewhere else.'

Maggie felt an unexpected lump of dread lodge somewhere at the base of her throat.

'He just likes to keep busy,' said Mr Harris with a shrug. 'It's always been the same. The boy can't sit still for two minutes together!'

Grabbing a damp cloth, Maggie began to sweep loose crumbs from the bar in an attempt to hide the wave of emotion. Hearing those words had hit harder than she'd anticipated. Of course, she knew that Luke wasn't a permanent resident on Crumcarey... but he'd done such a lovely job of his barn, she'd dared to hope that perhaps this visit might be a longer one than usual.

'Don't worry, I'm sure he'll make sure you're comfy at the cottage before he disappears,' said Mr Harris.

Maggie nodded and forced a small smile, but that had been the last thing on her mind.

'And if there's more to do, I'm sure we might be able to persuade him to come back next summer!' added Mr Harris brightly.

The words hit her like a lead weight in the centre of the chest. In fact, it was a miracle she was still standing.

Next summer?

That felt like an awfully long way away. She might have only met Luke a few days ago… but somehow, she couldn't imagine life on the island without him around.

Suddenly, the winter loomed ahead of her – long, cold and lonely. The prospect wasn't even remotely tempting.

'Ah, now lass,' said Mr Harris, his voice turning softer, laced with a gentle kindness as he watched her closely. 'You mustn't worry. Luke's here for now – so… let's make the most of him, shall we?'

Maggie smiled at her friend and was horrified to find that her lips were trembling with emotion. Mr Harris reached out, and this time he was the one to take *her* hand and give it a squeeze.

'Can I buy you a coffee?' she said, her voice thick. 'And maybe a pastry?'

'Why not, that would be grand,' said Mr Harris, smiling at her. 'Might as well be caffeinated enough to fly the truck home!'

'Now then, now then,' said Olive, reappearing from the back. 'Here's a diary for you Maggie, and a pack of dragons, a pack of unicorns, and I even found one pack of yellow duck stickers too!'

'Thank you!' said Maggie, placing Mr Harris's third breakfast in front of him and then grabbing a pen, ready to start filling the little book with as many of the names and dates as she could remember. 'Any chance you two will give me a hand – I think I've forgotten half of it already!'

'Swimming group!' said Olive, pointing at the next meeting date as Maggie flipped through the pages to the current month. 'Use one of the ducks!'

'Ducks?!' spluttered Mr Harris. 'You need sharks, girl!'

Maggie laughed and promptly did as she was told - drawing a tiny shark next to the note. Mr Harris nodded his approval as he tucked into his pastry.

CHAPTER 18

LUKE

*L*uke dangled his legs over the low wall, swinging them as he waited for his uncle to reappear with Maggie. The old man had insisted on picking her up from work so that Luke could finish fixing up the bit of guttering Sue Harcus had sent for the back of Pear Tree Cottage.

The guttering wasn't the only surprise the pair of them had cooked up for Maggie today. Between them, he and his uncle had managed to fit the mad, swirly carpet. Then Luke had finished all the pipework for the wood burner's back boiler.

He'd just set out the new windows where they would be fitted – but he'd run out of time for that particular job today. Not that that was a bad thing – he wanted to check Maggie was happy with them before they became a permanent fixture. After all, this wasn't his place, and the last thing Luke wanted was for her to feel like he was taking over. That wasn't the point of all this – plus, it sounded a bitch too much like Russell for his liking.

The final surprise - the icing on the cake as far as Luke was concerned - was the new sofa. It had come from Ray at Crum House. Apparently, it was one of the few bits of furniture his brother hadn't stolen and sold off while Ray had been travelling. Either way, it was a beauty. Sure, it was a bit lumpy, old and saggy… but it was wonderfully snuggly and comfortable. Luke knew this for a fact because he'd taken a five-minute catnap on it in between jobs.

Thankfully, Ray had helped to load it into the truck and had gladly hopped in for the ride to help unload it at the cottage, too. It was just as well, as there was no way Luke would have managed the heavy old thing with just his uncle's help!

The sofa had only just squeezed down the narrow hallway, and there had been much giggling and yelling of the word *PIVOT!* before it finally reached its destination in the open-plan living room.

Luke had left it plopped right in the middle of the space for the time being. It would be up to Maggie to choose where she wanted it.

'Speak of the devil,' he murmured, a broad grin spreading over his face as Mr Harris's truck turned into the driveway. Luke leapt down off the wall and did his best to ignore the funny little backflip his heart performed as Maggie climbed down from the

A FRESH START ON CRUMCAREY

passenger seat. She was clearly still mid-gossip with his uncle.

These little heart flips were fast becoming a regular thing... and Luke wasn't entirely sure what to do about them. He liked Maggie. She was gentle and kind and funny and brave. She was also so beautiful that she quite literally took his breath away.

Then there was the fact that she already felt like family – which was ridiculous, considering they'd known each other for less than a week.

Still... there was no way he could do anything about the weird, longing sensation in his chest. It wouldn't be fair on her. She'd already been stranded on the island by one bloke. There was no way he was going to be responsible for history repeating itself.

'Hi!' said Maggie, turning to him with a sunny smile.

'Good day?' said Luke, quickly tucking his troublesome thoughts away in his pocket. He'd stick to the practicalities of back boilers and guttering for now – they were safe and reliable and didn't threaten to land him in trouble at every turn.

'Brilliant day, thanks,' said Maggie. 'I think I've got my social calendar mapped out for the next six months!'

'She had to get a new diary and everything,' said Mr Harris. 'No shark stickers though.'

'Erm... shark stickers?' said Luke.

'Long story,' chuckled Maggie. 'I can't believe you're here again.

'Again?' said Mr Harris. 'The boy's been here all day!'

'Hush!' muttered Luke, shaking his head at his uncle.

'All day? Luke, I'm so sorry! I never meant to make so much trouble for you,' said Maggie, looking horrified.

'Rubbish,' said Luke.

'Aye, that it is,' said Mr Harris. 'He's happy as a pig in sh—'

'Shall I show you what we've been up to?' said Luke, shooting Maggie a lopsided grin.

'Great!' said Maggie.

'I'm going to head back to the farm,' said Mr Harris, with a small smile as he shot a wink at Luke. 'I've got... erm... cows to brush!'

Maggie raised her eyebrows, and Luke shrugged. As much as he was grateful for his uncle's unexpected tact in giving him a bit of time alone with her... could he not have come up with a slightly more believable excuse to make himself scarce?!

∽

'You're kidding me?!' gasped Maggie, staring at the sofa.

Luke grinned. Suddenly, all the swearing and

sweating as he and Ray had strong-armed the heavy bit of furniture into the cottage was more than worth it.

'Nope – all yours,' he said, smiling at her obvious excitement. 'The old one's beyond repair, I'm afraid. I wasn't sure what you wanted to do with it…?'

'Burn it?' laughed Maggie.

'That's doable,' said Luke. 'It's mostly wood, anyway.'

'This is amazing,' breathed Maggie.

'So… the next question is - where do you want it?' said Luke. 'I didn't want to decide for you – obviously!' he added quickly.

'I don't want to be too much trouble…' said Maggie again.

'Hush!' chuckled Luke. 'You might as well make the most of me while you've got me here.'

Luke caught a small flinch as some kind of emotion he couldn't quite place flashed across her face. It was gone as fast as it had appeared, and before he could wonder if he'd said something wrong, a bright smile reappeared on her face.

'In that case, I'm not sure,' said Maggie. 'The carpet looks even better than I imagined… so now's definitely the time to change things up a bit! What do you think? Where would you put it?'

'Well… you've got some options,' said Luke. 'Wait just a sec.'

Grabbing one end of the bulky sofa, he dragged it

over towards one of the walls, before dropping it in place and waiting for her verdict.

She didn't say anything.

'So, this is option one!' he prompted.

Holding up one finger, Luke executed an elaborate dive into the cushions before striking a pose. With his head resting on one hand, he grinned at her as he lifted one leg in the air, doing his best to point his toes like a ballet dancer.

Maggie snorted with laughter.

'You'd get the dappled light in the mornings – streaming in through the window and hitting you while you enjoy your breakfast,' he said, putting on a posh accent and pretending he was presenting an interiors TV show.

'Dappled light?' chuckled Maggie.

'Okay, you're going to have to use your imagination until I've had the chance to get rid of those boards and fix that window,' said Luke, reverting to his normal voice as he struggled to sit up. 'What do you think?'

Maggie cocked her head. 'Hmm… maybe… but it's not quite right.'

'Okie dokey… how about this then…'

Luke got to his feet and towed the sofa in a semi-circle until it had its back to the window so that it was now facing the wall. Once again, he bounced down into the cushions, this time grabbing an imaginary remote control and pointing it at the wall.

'Just imagine a fifty-two-inch flat-screen TV right

there,' said Luke. 'Chillax and watch non-stop adverts and those appalling mini-series back to back!'

Maggie shook her head, looking horrified.

'No?' he said, fluttering his eyelashes innocently at her.

'A *definite* no to the TV,' she laughed. 'And I don't fancy staring at a blank wall either!'

'Thank heavens for that,' said Luke. 'Alright, gimmie a hand for the next one?'

Maggie nodded. 'Where are we going.'

'Swing it around to you?' said Luke.

Maggie dragged one end in a wide arc while Luke lifted the other and angled it towards the wood burner.

'There?' she said, stepping back to take a look.

'Let me model it for you!' said Luke, shooting her a grin before pulling on his poker face. Then he raised his arms above his head like an Olympic diver and leapt onto the lumpy cushions. Milking it for all it was worth, he turned to face Maggie, arms and legs akimbo.

'I like it!' she chuckled.

'You wait till you've tried it!' he said with a wink, waggling his eyebrows and patting the cushion next to him with an exaggerated invitation.

Maggie didn't hesitate. Throwing herself down onto the sofa next to him, she let out a contented little sigh that instantly made Luke's heart do a triple-turn and dive of its own.

Breathing slowly, he did his best to relax… and let

his arm fall across her shoulders. Maggie snuggled into him.

'You're right,' she sighed. 'I needed to test it out for myself.'

She glanced up at him and Luke suddenly felt like he couldn't breathe… like he couldn't look away from her.

'Definitely a good sofa,' said Maggie. 'Not bad company, either.'

'Mm-hmm,' said Luke as her face inched towards him.

He couldn't look away. Their faces were close. Very close. Suddenly, it felt like she was a magnet and he was utterly helpless - caught in her field, speeding towards her. He couldn't pull away… even though he knew he should.

'I guess we'd better sort out the rest of the room,' he said, his voice low.

'I think the rest of the room can wait,' said Maggie with a small smile, before closing the gap between them.

CHAPTER 19

MAGGIE

For the first time since she'd started her new job, The Tallyaff was empty. Maggie knew she should be glad of a few minutes of peace and quiet to catch up with restocking the little shop – but right now, she could really do with the flurry of a busy ferry run to get her out of her own head.

'No such luck,' she muttered, grabbing a large box of crisps and starting to re-fill the racks.

The ferry and flights had a different schedule today, and they weren't expecting any visitors for at least an hour or so. Unfortunately, it was giving Maggie far too much time to chase herself around inside her own head... and she felt like she was spiralling in ever-decreasing circles around a plughole of doom.

She'd kissed Luke.
And... it had been amazing.
More than amazing.

Gah!

It hadn't been one of those kisses where they'd broken apart and realised they really shouldn't be doing what they were doing. Nothing like it, in fact.

They'd kissed and kissed and then kissed again. They'd barely paused to take a breath - ending up wedged on her new sofa in a tangle of limbs and pushed-up jumpers.

That sofa was most definitely going to be her favourite spot in the whole cottage if that sort of thing happened on it on a regular basis!

'And there's the rub,' she muttered, hurling one crip packet after another into the waiting basket. It would be a miracle if she wasn't smashing them all to smithereens – but there was something satisfying about the *whoosh-crunch* each packet made as it pelted into the target.

'Tell me,' said Olive, appearing at her side and quietly removing the box of crisps from her reach before she could ruin them all, 'is it all crisps you hate, or do you have something against Firecracker Prawn in particular?'

'Sorry,' muttered Maggie, placing the remaining pack she was holding gently into the basket.

Olive chuckled. 'I think you need a break.'

'No I—' started Maggie.

'Okay, let me try that again,' said Olive wrapping an arm around her shoulders and steering her out of the shop and over towards the bar. '*I* need a break, and I'm making us a drink. As your boss, you will sit down with me and tell me if you like the way I make hot chocolate.'

'Hot chocolate?' said Maggie, mildly surprised that it wasn't going to be one of Olive's classic triple shot coffees.

'Yes… because something tells me you need a dash of comfort this morning,' said Olive. 'And the smashed crisps tell me you *definitely* don't need any more caffeine!'

'Fair point,' laughed Maggie, feeling the tight band of worry give way a little under the beam of Olive's friendship.

'So… what's got you all riled up?' said Olive, grabbing a block of dark chocolate and starting to grate it into a dish with swift sure, strokes as Maggie climbed up onto a bar stool.

'Luke,' said Maggie, his name slipping out of her mouth before she'd even thought to put any filters in place. But then, this was Olive. The woman was kindness personified. Plus – she had a knack for getting to the bottom of things, so there wasn't much point in beating around the bush.

'Oh yes?' said Olive blandly.

'I kissed him,' muttered Maggie. 'Or… well… we kissed,'

'Mr Harris is going to be over the moon,' said Olive, smiling at her.

'Huh?' said Maggie. That was the last thing she'd been expecting.

'He's been waiting for one of you to make a move,' said Olive, adding cinnamon to her concoction. 'Ever since he found you wearing Luke's underpants!'

'I was using them as pyjamas!' said Maggie, for what felt like the thousandth time.

'Yeah, yeah, so you keep saying,' said Olive with a naughty wink. 'Anyway, what's the problem? Bad kisser?'

'The opposite,' said Maggie with a little sigh.

'Soo... you're just not feeling it?'

Maggie raised an eyebrow. She wasn't going to confirm or deny whether she'd felt *it*, or anything else!

'No! I didn't mean...!' hooted Olive. 'I *meant*, did you change your mind when you kissed him? Do you just want to be friends? Wished you'd stuck to the house renovations?'

'No to all of the above,' said Maggie, resting her chin on her hands.

'Alright, I can't help you if you don't tell me what's going on,' said Olive, straightening up and fixing her with a stern expression.

'I liked it,' she said, 'and that's the understatement of the century.'

Maggie paused, wondering how much to say. She shot a glance over her shoulder to double-check that the pair of them were still alone. The last thing she needed was for Mr Harris to overhear her working through her muddled feelings. Or – heaven forbid – Luke himself!

With a deep breath, Maggie decided she was all in.

'I loved it,' she said quietly. 'Best kiss of my life.' She wrapped her arms around herself, wishing it was Luke hugging her.

'Well, that's wonderful… isn't it?' said Olive, looking confused.

Maggie shrugged. 'Mr Harris mentioned something to me. Something about Luke.'

'Uh huh?' said Olive,

'He said Luke doesn't stay put anywhere for long,' she said. 'He doesn't settle and that… well… that he'll be off before we know it. Mr Harris reckons he won't be back until next summer…' she trailed off.

Maggie knew she was being ridiculous. It had just been a kiss, after all.

A kiss that had the power to rock the foundations of her entire life.

Sucking in a deep breath, Maggie gave herself a mental slap for getting all *dramatic* over a boy.

'Well, I *can* understand where you're coming from,' said Olive gently.

'You can?' said Maggie, feeling a strange rush of relief. Maybe she wasn't being quite as big a drama lama as she thought.

'Of course!' said Olive. 'You've told me a bit about your ex, and I've seen your face when those postcards arrive. It's not surprising you don't want to get yourself right back into the same situation with someone else.'

'Luke's nothing like Russell,' said Maggie, instantly jumping to his defence.

Olive grinned at her. 'Obviously not, and he's put a beautiful smile on your face these last few days. I'm sorry to say it, but I don't think Russell did that even when he was living here.'

'What should I do, Olive?' said Maggie, begging for an answer that wouldn't break her heart.

Olive shook her head slowly. 'Here's the thing – I don't have any answers for you. I've known Luke since he was a little boy, and he's always been the same. It's just like Mr Harris told you. It's not that he has itchy feet… more like he's just not found anything big enough to hold him in the one place for very long.'

'Is that different?' said Maggie.

'I'd say so,' said Olive. 'I guess what you need to ask yourself is… exactly how do you feel about Luke?'

Maggie shook her head. 'It's all so new, I can't say. But… it feels like… it *could* be that big. In time.'

'Then… I guess my answer is… maybe you're taking all this a bit too seriously.' Olive shrugged. 'It's always a complicated thing, starting something new with someone you barely know. If you want my advice?'

'So much!' groaned Maggie.

'Then I'd say - just relax and let things happen naturally instead of asking all these big questions one day after you've shared your first kiss!'

A FRESH START ON CRUMCAREY

Maggie nodded slowly and then started to laugh. 'I'm such an idiot.'

'Oh no you're not,' said Olive stoutly. 'Definitely not. When you meet someone who turns your whole life around in the space of a few seconds, all bets are off. But... give it a chance. It might turn out to be nothing.'

Maggie crinkled her nose. She didn't like the sound of that much.

'Or,' said Olive, popping a huge cup of cream-filled, cinnamon-scented hot chocolate in front of her, 'or... it might turn out to be something very special indeed.'

'I like that version a lot better,' said Maggie with a grin, wrapping both hands around the mug and letting the warmth and scent calm her senses. 'Thanks, Olive.'

'Cheers,' said Olive with a wink, taking a long sip of her own drink.

Maggie took a sip too, then let out a long sigh. Olive was right. She'd come very close to acting like a lovesick teenager after one kiss with a boy she liked. In her defence, though, it *had* been a long time since she'd had any romance in her life... if you didn't count the idiot who kept sending her postcards from all over the world, of course – and she *definitely* didn't count him.

It was time to look to the future – but she needed to do that one day at a time. She'd only just discovered the wonderful community on Crumcarey, after all. She'd have found them far sooner if she hadn't been brooding over Russell and convinced that she had to face the world alone.

Now… whatever happened… she'd never be alone again. She was part of Crumcarey – and that was a relationship she was excited to explore.

CHAPTER 20

LUKE

*P*ausing just inside the door of The Tallyaff, Luke watched Maggie as she chatted with Anna McCluskey. He'd spent all day desperate to talk to her again... to see her again... and now she seemed to have robbed him of the power of movement.

The kiss last night had haunted him all day. It hadn't helped that he'd been working at Pear Tree Cottage again. Every time he caught a glimpse of Maggie's new-old sofa facing the wood burner, his spine tingled with anticipation... which was stupid, because *she* might not want to revisit the moment.

He did though. Very much. Preferably, as soon as humanly possible!

Luke had driven himself practically insane with mental images from the night before as he'd fixed Maggie's new windows in place. They'd flooded the little cottage with more light than the poor old place had seen for months... and he hoped she'd like it. He hoped all the changes would help her feel like the place was hers... and like she could truly settle and call it home.

As for him... Maggie had turned his world upside down in just a few short days. He'd thought he had a plan. Come to Crumcarey, spend time with Uncle Harris and help out wherever he was needed until the ferry refit was done and dusted. Then he'd be off to explore somewhere new.

Well... that plan was well and truly wrecked!

Last night had left him feeling both scattered and completely grounded. Maggie had blown everything he thought he knew about himself to pieces, leaving his feet planted in Crumcarey's sandy soil in a way they'd never been before.

That hadn't been a *normal* kiss... there had been some kind of magic at work, he was sure of it.

Maybe that's why he'd completely forgotten to tell Maggie about the drawing with the ice cream spatter, and Stella and Frank's request for her to redesign their cottage for them. They had a lot to talk about, that was for sure!

'Luke!' cried Olive, beaming at him as she appeared through the doorway that led to the rooms upstairs.

Maggie's head whipped up at the sound of his name, and for a brief moment, her eyes gleamed at him with undisguised joy... before a hint of confusion muscled its way in.

'Hi Olive,' he said. 'Sorry, I'm here a bit early for Maggie... but I'll wait.'

'You're here for me?' said Maggie, her confusion turning to worry. 'Is Mr Harris okay?'

'He's fine!' said Luke, feeling decidedly warm and fuzzy about the fact that she clearly adored the salty old gent as much as he did. 'Exhausted from bossing the pair of us around all week, I think. He's chilling back at the farmhouse this evening.'

'Phew, okay good,' said Maggie with a nod. 'I was worried I was causing him a bit too much trouble.'

'Rubbish,' chuckled Olive. 'That man's middle name is trouble. Fancy using your uncle as an excuse to pick up our Maggie!'

Luke felt the prickle of a blush spread across his forehead, and he grinned sheepishly at Maggie.

'Fine,' he huffed. 'I muscled in because I wanted to be the one to come and steal you away for the night.'

He watched as Maggie turned a delicate shade of beetroot, shooting an embarrassed glance at Anna. Anna let out a delighted squeal.

'I'll leave you lot to it,' she said. 'You wait till I tell Ray that Little Miss Independent here has tamed the beast!'

'Tamed?' squeaked Maggie, shaking her head and turning an even deeper shade of red – if such a thing was possible.

'Beast?' gasped Luke in mock outrage.

Bang went any hope of keeping his intentions

towards Maggie on the down-low! Now it would be all over the island before they'd even left The Tallyaff.

'Well, as you manned up and admitted it, I guess you can steal your girl away five minutes early,' said Olive.

'I'm not...' started Maggie.

'She's not...' muttered Luke.

'Okay, okay – just – shoo!' chuckled Olive, handing Maggie her bag from behind the bar and then making ushering motions at the pair of them.

'Sorry about that,' muttered Maggie, as they tumbled out through the door into the car park.

Luke shrugged his shoulders. 'It's Olive. I'm used to it!'

They both fell silent for a long beat, and Luke realised he was digging the tip of one grubby work boot into the gravel like a nervous schoolboy.

'Erm... so...' said Maggie, glancing at the truck and then back to him.

'Sorry for dragging you away early,' said Luke.

'Don't apologise for that!' said Maggie. 'I'm more than done for one day.'

'Long one?' said Luke.

'Oh yes!' said Maggie.

Luke waited, but when it became clear she wasn't about to elaborate any further, he ran his fingers through his hair, trying to muster the courage to set the next part of his plan in action.

'So... I've got an idea... if you're up for it,' said Luke.

'Ooh, intriguing,' said Maggie, her eyes sparkling with curiosity.

'Let's hop in the truck and I'll explain as we go,' he said. 'As long as you don't need to head straight home?'

'Nope – I'm up for it!' said Maggie, looking excited. 'Though, this is all very cloak and dagger. What are you up to, Luke Harris?'

Luke grinned at her. He liked the way she said his name. He liked the fact that she was excited to go along with his hair-brained plan without knowing what it was, even though she must be completely knackered from a long day at work.

Hell... he just *liked* her. Everything about her.

Luke let out a breath and returned her grin. Suddenly, this didn't feel risky, or stupid, or way out of midfield. It just felt right.

'Ready for a magical mystery tour of Crumcarey?' he asked, pulling on his seatbelt before turning to meet her bright eyes.

'Always!'

~

They drove in companionable silence for a good ten minutes, and Luke took the road that led up to the cliffs where the puffins hung out in the summer. They were all gone now, of course, but that didn't matter. It wasn't the cheeky little birds he was taking Maggie to see.

'Nearly there,' he said, shooting her a smile as he turned down a rough track.

Once upon a time, he imagined it would have been carefully tended, its potholes filled once a year and the hump in the centre scraped back. Now, though, there was a good chance they'd both need to visit a chiropractor after bouncing down the narrow, rutted path.

'Where on earth are you taking me?' giggled Maggie, bouncing around in her seat and eyeballing the sad-looking cottage at the end of the lane.

'Welcome to Peedie Croft,' said Luke.

'O-kay…' said Maggie slowly, turning to stare at him.

'Come on – let's have a poke around!' he said, not quite ready to let her in on his plan just yet. He wanted to see what she had to say without confusing her with all the details.

Maggie shrugged and hopped out of the car, grabbing a bobble hat from her jacket pocket and pulling it on to stop her long hair from going crazy in the wind.

'How long's this place been empty?' she said, craning her neck.

'As far as I know, at least forty years,' said Luke, leading the way to peer through one of the windows.

Maggie followed him eagerly. After a brief look, she peeled away and wandered towards the overgrown walled garden at the back.

'What do you think of the place?' he said, following her.

'It must have been lovely once,' she said. 'Hey, can we go inside?'

'Sure!' said Luke.

It didn't take them long to look around. The cottage was completely dilapidated, but that's not what Luke saw in front of him... all he could think about was his plan.

'So... what would you do with it?' he said lightly, as they made their way back outside. He'd done his best to make it sound like a throwaway question, but he had a feeling he'd just failed miserably.

Maggie raised an eyebrow at him. 'What do you mean?'

'I mean... if it was yours to renovate, what would you do?'

She went quiet for a moment, staring at the old place thoughtfully. 'Do you have a pen and paper in the truck?'

'I might have an old napkin?' said Luke.

'Better than nothing!' laughed Maggie.

'You keep thinking and I'll grab it for you,' said Luke.

Five minutes later, Maggie had drawn a stunning sketch of Peedie Croft in the middle of a piece of kitchen roll. Around the edges, she'd added smaller sketches, outlining new features that could turn the shell of the old place into something rather lovely.

Luke shook his head, completely blown away by the sheer talent Maggie had been sitting on for so long.

'I mean... this is seriously rough,' she said, adding a few arrows to the drawing before popping the cap back on the biro. 'Of course, it would all depend on what it was going to be used for. A porch is a good starting point though – kind of essential up here!'

'And you've added more windows along the west wall to make the most of this beautiful evening sunlight and the views over the cliffs,' said Luke, half mesmerised by the drawing, and half by the way the sunlight was weaving golden highlights into the ends of Maggie's hair.

'Exactly,' said Maggie, peering at her sketch again. 'So... what's the plan?' she added curiously.

'I'll tell you at the next place!' said Luke, grabbing her hand and towing her back towards the truck.

CHAPTER 21

MAGGIE

'Ready for the next one?'

Luke was grinning at her and bouncing on the balls of his feet like an excited toddler, but Maggie held up her hand to stop him in his tracks - then started to laugh when he stuck out his bottom lip in an exaggerated pout.

'As fascinating as it's been to traipse all over Crumcarey looking at derelict spiles of stone in the evening sunshine,' she said, digging her heels in as he tried to draw her playfully towards the truck, 'you seem to have forgotten that I've got my own pile of stones waiting for me at home.'

Luke grinned, but Maggie crossed her arms. She wasn't going to be swayed just because her knees trembled every time he threw that high-voltage smile at her. She had a feeling there was more to this magical mystery tour than introducing her to hidden corners of the island.

Every single place Luke had taken her to visit had been uninhabited and in a state of disrepair… and now Maggie wanted to know what he was up to. As much as it had been fun having her brain squeezed for ideas about what she'd do with each of the buildings, it was time for him to clue her in.

'Come on, out with it,' she said, 'what are you up to? What's this really about?'

'Well,' said Luke, 'I want to know if you're interested.'

Maggie raised both eyebrows at that. 'Interested in what, exactly? Come on Luke Harris, you're being very mysterious and it doesn't suit you!'

Luke let out a hoot of laughter. 'Well… I've had this idea…' he paused and ran his fingers through his hair. If she didn't know any better, Maggie would guess that he was nervous - but for the life of her, she couldn't imagine why.

'Look,' he continued, 'I know this is a bit out of the blue… but I want to renovate some of these old ruins.'

'You do?' said Maggie in surprise.

'I do. With you.'

'With me?' she parroted.

Luke laughed and then nodded.

'I want us to team up – your mad, amazing design skills and my odd-jobbery… and Uncle Harris's ability to sniff out or scrounge all the goodies we need to get

A FRESH START ON CRUMCAREY

each job done,' said Luke. 'With permission, of course. I think we'd make a great team.'

'But... I... you...?' Maggie spluttered, trying to take it all in. So it *definitely* hadn't been a random evening pottering around the island, then. 'But... why?' said Maggie.

A little flower of hope had suddenly lifted its head. Did this mean he wanted to stay on Crumcarey?

'The island's turning a corner,' he said. 'Everyone's been saying it. With Ray's dive school and the new runway at the airport. Then there's the publicity around the standing stones...'

'I heard they're fake?' said Maggie.

'Shhhh!' said Luke, rushing to her side and placing a hand over her mouth, looking around him with exaggerated care.

Maggie giggled and shoved his hand away.

'I will neither confirm nor deny such rumours,' muttered Luke. 'Either way, it doesn't stop the tourists turning up, does it?'

'True,' agreed Maggie.

'Olive hasn't got enough rooms for them all at The Tallyaff,' continued Luke. 'She's been turning bookings away all summer.'

'Also true,' said Maggie, 'and the conference centre...' she trailed off delicately, scrunching up her nose.

'Until Joyce either sorts that place out or sells up, it's not really fit for purpose,' sighed Luke. 'Plus, it's full all the time anyway, with those poor archaeology students!'

Luke shook his head and waved a hand impatiently at himself, clearly irritated that he'd wandered off topic.

'Anyway, the point is, loads more visitors are discovering the island. The more people we can get to spend time on Crumcarey, the better. The right ones fall in love with the place – they always do – and then they want to come back. I want to give them places to come back *to!*'

'Mr Harris is going to *hate* this,' chuckled Maggie, imagining the impending grumbling about traffic and campervans.

'On the contrary,' said Luke, shaking his head. 'He's all in! He's really enjoyed having something to focus on over the last few days while we've been working on your place... and I think he likes having family around.'

Maggie swallowed. Part of her barely dared to believe what she was hearing.

'I'm sorry,' said Luke. 'I know all of this is a bit sudden, but it's kind of how my brain works.'

'It's... that's... don't apologise!' said Maggie, her mind churning with a mixture of possibility and excitement, and fear and doubt. 'I mean... do you have the capital to buy all these places? Are they even for sale?'

'They've been empty for decades,' said Luke with a shrug. 'There's a byelaw here that means they revert to being owned by the community if they sit empty for long enough.'

'What does that mean?' she said. 'Practically, I mean?'

'It means we need to get Olive on side,' said Luke. 'But I don't think there's any worry there. She's head of tourism - and basically everything else too. I'm sure she'll be on board. Having more places for people to stay would be good for the economy. I don't want to sound too hard-headed - I just think we have an opportunity to do something really special here... to bring these corners of Crumcarey back to life.'

Maggie had been nodding slowly while Luke had been talking, and she could feel the beginnings of pure excitement in the pit of her stomach. The chance to bring these lovely old places back to life? She'd loved to be involved!

But... she dreaded to think what Russell would say. Probably that she didn't have the imagination *or* the skill.

Maggie shook her head irritably. It wasn't up to him, was it? Not anymore. This was *her* life now. Maybe even hers *and* Luke's... *if* he was going to stay. But it was like Olive said, she needed to give it time...

'I need to think about it,' she said. 'Is that okay?'

'Of course,' said Luke, shooting her a warm smile, even though Maggie suspected she saw a tiny hint of disappointment that she wasn't jumping for joy and diving in head first.

'Can... can you drive me home?' she said in a small voice.

'Sure,' said Luke with a little nod.

'Hey Luke?' she said, reaching out and threading her fingers gently through his.

'Yeah?' he said, crooking one eyebrow at her.

'Thanks for the magical mystery tour,' she said, pulling him in and planting a light kiss on his lips as the sun gleamed golden across the sea.

∼

Luke had dropped Maggie off at the front of the cottage, and as hard as it had been not to beg him to accompany her inside, Maggie hadn't been joking when she'd said she needed to think.

Her head was full and her imagination was ablaze... especially after Luke had told her about Stella and Frank's reactions to her drawings on the way home. She needed an evening on her own to let her mind wander through all the new possibilities that had appeared at her feet.

Popping the kettle on, Maggie padded around the cottage, admiring her new windows. It was already growing dark outside, and she couldn't wait to experience their full effect in the morning. Right now, though, she had something she wanted to do.

Dashing through to the bedroom, Maggie hunted until she found the plastic box where she'd stashed her

A FRESH START ON CRUMCAREY

good drawing paper and her fine liners. Making her way back out into the living room, she popped her supplies down onto her lovely new kitchen table.

'Strong coffee first,' she said, spooning grounds into a cafetiere and then pouring herself a huge mug of the stuff to keep her going. Then she flicked on the various lamps she'd been gifted to get as much light as possible, before settling down at the table. She needed to unload her overflowing imagination before she burst with ideas, and this was the best way she knew how.

Fidgeting in her chair for a second, she reached into her pocket and pulled out the crumpled piece of kitchen roll Luke had given her back at Peedie Croft, along with two or three more she'd pilfered to make notes about the other places.

The sketches were scrappy beyond belief, but they were exactly what she needed to jog her memory. Picking up her favourite pen for the first time in forever, Maggie un-clicked the cap and then paused for a long moment with the nib hovering over the clean sheet of paper.

With a deep breath, she started to draw.

Peedie Croft came first, and then Maggie worked her way through the other houses they'd visited in turn. She'd always been good with remembering details, and it wasn't long before she had immaculate sketches of the buildings as they stood now, surrounded by design ideas she'd love to bring to life.

Russell had hated it when she'd gone through this

process for Pear Tree Cottage. He'd resented the fact that she had the ability to imagine the project as a finished whole. For all his talk about wanting to work on their home together, he'd turned out to be a weird mixture of control freak and completely useless when it came down to anything practical.

Maggie paused for a long moment, frowning as she lifted her nib from the drawing of the final cottage they'd visited. Did she *really* want to get involved in this? To tie herself up with yet more dilapidated parts of Crumcarey that needed more care and attention than she could possibly give them? What if she ended up with it all landing on her shoulders? She couldn't take that again.

'No. This is Luke,' she muttered, shaking her head. 'He's not Russell. He's *nothing* like Russell.'

Reaching for a sip of coffee, Maggie laughed, realising that she must have drained the mug hours ago. She really ought to think about going to bed… but she wasn't quite finished yet. She had a decision to make before she could go to sleep, and it wasn't something to be taken lightly.

Did she want to dive into this hair-brained plan with Luke – a man she barely knew?

'But I *do* know him!' she muttered. She might not have known him long, but she knew his heart. There was no side to Luke Harris. He was adventure personified… and kindness, hard work, and warm kisses on the sofa.

A FRESH START ON CRUMCAREY

Maggie shivered and let her eyes drift over the table bearing page after page of drawings, full of plans and ideas. Every single cottage had its own special character. These places were more than a sum of their slightly decrepit parts. The views, the mountains, the coastlines, the gardens – each cottage had its own unique blend of all these things. Maggie could just imagine them coming back to life and delighting anyone who visited.

Yawning widely, Maggie scrubbed at her eyes and glanced at the clock on her kitchen wall.

Wow... midnight?!

No wonder her stomach was growling - she'd completely lost track of time. She'd also run out of paper.

She needed something to eat.

She needed to sleep.

She needed to talk to Luke!

CHAPTER 22

LUKE

A cool breeze kissed Luke's cheeks, and he let out a long, blissed-out sigh. He must have forgotten to close the curtains around the bed last night. He turned over on his mattress with his eyes still shut fast. The fresh air seemed to be coming from that direction, and it smelled decidedly like autumn… and something else… something sweet…

Twitching his nostrils, he took a deep breath and then yawned. Maybe it was time to get up…? Then again… maybe not quite yet. Ten more minutes.

Snuggling down into his duvet, Luke let out another contented sigh as he kicked one long leg free of the bedding… and then went dead still as a strange sound caught his attention.

Was that… a giggle?

Opening his eyes a crack, he spotted a slender silhouette framed against the morning light flooding in through the barn's open front door. Long, dark hair framed a look of admiration on Maggie's lovely face.

'Mags?' he mumbled.

'Yep!' she said, sounding decidedly cheerful.

Blinking away the last traces of sleep and slipping one arm beneath his head, Luke peered at her, not quite believing she was actually there. But no, it was definitely Maggie… looking as stunning as usual. She had a pen tucked behind one ear and a grin fixed firmly on her face.

'How long have you been there?' he said.

'Long enough to learn that you don't wear anything to bed!' she said, wiggling her eyebrows at him.

'Hmm,' said Luke, wondering if he should be embarrassed about this discovery. Then he decided against it. After all, she *was* standing in the open door of *his* home! 'Just for the record,' he said, 'it's Saturday morning. That's the only reason I'm still in bed.'

'Day off?' said Maggie. 'I didn't know Luke Harris understood the concept!'

'I've barely had a break since I arrived.' Luke gave an exaggerated huff, feigning a grump that he promptly spoiled by breaking into a wide smile. 'You know, what with all the uninvited guests turning up in the middle of the night, looking like drowned rats and then forcing me to sleep on the sofa…'

'You definitely weren't forced,' she chuckled. 'Besides, if I'd have known there was plenty of room in that bed of yours for two people…'

Maggie trailed off, and Luke felt the magic of her words light a fire in him. He gulped, making sure the duvet was still firmly in place and covering him properly.

'Of course, there were the days of hard physical labour after that, too,' he joked, trying to cover the effect this beautiful woman was having on him.

'Yeah… I guess you deserve a bit of a lie-in, then,' said Maggie, taking a step inside the barn and closing the door behind her.

Luke knew this should make him feel less exposed… but now it was just the pair of them. He swallowed hard, looking for something to say to take his mind off his racing heart.

'What have you got there?' he said, nodding at the pile of papers she had cuddled protectively against her chest. Of course, he had a good idea of what they might be. New drawings.

'Does… does this mean…' he started.

'I've got a couple of questions before I show you these,' she said, cutting across him. The words had poured out in a rush as though she'd been holding them in.

'Sure,' he said easily. 'Ask me anything.'

'What you told me last night… does it mean you're planning on sticking around?' she said. 'At least… at least for a bit?'

Luke smiled. Mainly because he'd had a feeling that

question might be coming. But also because it meant she cared enough to ask it.

'I am. It does,' said Luke. 'I'm staying on Crumcarey. Permanently.'

He watched as Maggie bit her lip, clearly holding something in… though he couldn't guess what.

'I've already told Uncle Harris,' he added, just for something to fill the taut silence between them. 'He's… well, he's thrilled,' he laughed, remembering the loud round of cheering followed by a resounding thump on the back as the old man had blinked back happy tears. Luke quickly swallowed hard as the memory brought a lump to his throat. 'I get to stay in the barn for free as long as I give him a hand with some of the work that needs doing on the farmhouse. I mean… I'd have done that either way – so, win-win!'

Maggie smiled at him and nodded. 'And… he knows about your plans…'

'Yep,' said Luke happily. 'Like I said, he's well up for it – as long as McGregor is invited, of course.'

Maggie nodded again, nibbling on her thumbnail as she stared at him. Luke shifted his weight. The suspense was killing him!

'Anything else?' he prompted.

'So… we're doing this?' she said. 'Together?'

'Yup,' Luke nodded. 'Or at least… that's what I want. Is it… is it what you want?'

'Depends. I've got one more question…' she said slowly. 'It's a two-parter…'

'Okay?' chuckled Luke, wondering what she had up her sleeve.

'You made that bed, right?' she said.

Luke nodded, raising an eyebrow.

'Is it strong enough to handle two of us?'

'Yes,' said Luke, the word coming out in husky surprise.

'Sure?'

'Questioning my workmanship already?' he laughed.

'You didn't answer my question,' said Maggie, taking one slow, deliberate step towards him.

'Why don't you try it and see?' said Luke.

Maggie nodded once. Then she wandered over towards the table and placed her bundle of drawings carefully down on the surface. Next, she drew the pen out from behind her ear – her movements excruciatingly slow.

Luke swallowed, watching her every move as though time had slowed to a near standstill. Then, with an excited squeal that took him by surprise, Maggie whirled around and dashed straight for him, diving right on top of him.

'See, didn't break!' Luke mumbled from beneath a tangle of dark hair and sweet kisses.

'I still think it needs further testing,' Maggie breathed into his neck.

Well, he wasn't going to complain about that!

CHAPTER 23

❦

MAGGIE

Maggie popped her paintbrush down and picked up her glass of apple juice, taking a deep swig. She was busy applying a lick of paint to the stonework around her brand-new windows – and considering it was the first week of October, it was weirdly warm.

'Gotta make the most of it, eh boy?' she said, glancing down at McGregor, who was sprawled out on the grass in the shade of the tarpaulin she'd strung up for him. The little dog didn't bother to raise his head, but he did give his tail a wag of acknowledgement before his eyes drifted closed again.

Luke was off in the truck – first to collect Mr Harris from his swimming session up at Crum House, and then the pair of them were off on a tour of the island to collect the latest batch of bits and bobs they'd been gifted.

Maggie couldn't believe how fast things were moving... not that she was complaining in the slightest. Still, it had only been a week since Luke had arranged a meeting with Olive after one of her shifts at The Tallyaff.

Over a meal, Luke had laid out his plans – and Maggie and Mr Harris had chipped in to help fill in the gaps. Olive had loved the idea and had happily volunteered to organise any paperwork required when it came to designating the buildings as community assets.

Just one week later, they were getting ready to make a start on Peedie Croft... and Maggie couldn't remember when she'd last been this busy – *or* this happy.

It wasn't just that part of the project that was moving forward, either. Word had got out about what they were up to – probably thanks to Stella and Frank bragging about the designs she'd pulled together for their cottage. They seemed to be showing the drawings to everyone who stopped for an ice cream.

The result of all this was that Maggie's diary was quickly filling with appointments to visit homes all over the island – and her sketchbook was most definitely invited too!

'Right, lad,' she said, stretching her back and popping her glass down. 'I've got two more things to do before we go get an ice cream, okay?'

McGregor was too fast asleep to reply… but that was okay.

'First things first,' she muttered, heading over towards the large, flat stone she'd earmarked for the first job. Hoisting it up onto the end of the low wall right next to the road, Maggie angled it until she was happy. Then she retrieved her paint can and brush from the windowsill.

It was time for the little cottage to cast off its idiotic name. Slowly but steadily, she daubed three words onto the stone.

No Trees Cottage

When she'd finished, she took a step back and nodded. There. Drawing inspiration from Mr Harris's mutterings, she'd re-christened *her* home with a name that was both rational and a little bit silly – just the way it should be.

Maggie was done with anything that reminded her of the struggles of the past. During their meeting at the Tallyaff, Olive had handed over a pile of post – and she'd unexpectedly received the closure she'd been missing ever since Russell had left the island.

A letter! An actual letter.

Maggie had been tempted just to bin the thing without reading it… but then curiosity had got the better of her and she'd wandered away from the table before tearing open the envelope.

Russell had moved into a tiny studio flat in New York. There wouldn't be any more postcards. He was getting married.

Maggie skimmed the first handful of sentences and then realised they meant absolutely nothing to her. With a shrug, she'd tossed the pages of full self-congratulation into The Tallyaff's roaring wood burner. Then she'd returned to the table to continue discussing plans for the future without so much as a backward glance.

'Come on then lad,' she said, patting her thigh until McGregor realised she was talking to him. The little dog slowly clambered to his feet and yawned. 'Let's go get that ice cream… I'll brainstorm the other job on the way.'

After helping him into the passenger seat of her dented car, Maggie climbed behind the wheel.

'All right, here we go,' she said.

Reversing out onto the road, Maggie blew out a long breath as she turned the car in the direction of Big Sandy. It didn't take long before she was frowning in concentration as her brain turned over the possibilities. It was the one thing they had left to organise – they needed a name for their new venture.

'Crumcarey Cottages?' she said, wrinkling her nose.

McGregor growled.

'Yeah, I know… rubbish,' she chuckled. 'How about Harris, Henderson and Harris?'

McGregor pawed at his nose, making her laugh.

A FRESH START ON CRUMCAREY

'Okay, okay, I get it,' she said. 'I'm guessing you like McGregor, Harris, Harris and Henderson better?'

McGregor gave a short, sharp bark and started wagging his tail.

'Alright – you've convinced me,' she tutted. 'I'm blaming you when we can't fit it on the business cards, though.'

Ten minutes later, they arrived at the beach. The parking spot was mercifully empty, so Maggie let McGregor out of the car and watched as he skipped gleefully down onto the sand to chase dried bits of seaweed.

'Well, if it isn't our little designer!' called Stella excitedly, waving her over to the ice cream van.

'Hi!' said Maggie. 'I've nearly finished those extra sketches for your place... do you fancy a drink at the Tally at the weekend to go over them?'

'I'd love that!' said Frank, grinning at her from the back of the van where he was mixing up a fresh batch of something that smelled like a combination of cherries and heaven.

'Me too,' said Stella. 'But... how about you come up to our place instead. I'll cook and then you can talk us through your ideas on-site!'

Maggie felt a dollop of something sweet settle in her stomach... and she hadn't even ordered an ice cream yet.

'And bring your boys with you too, if you'd like?' said Stella.

'My boys?' laughed Maggie.

'Yeah,' chuckled Stella.

'Now... who on earth would they be?'

Stella grinned and pointed over Maggie's shoulder. She turned, only to find Luke and Mr Harris striding down the sand dune towards her with identical grins on their faces. McGregor pelted up from the beach to greet them, his tail wagging frantically.

'Oi, you two slackers!' she called to them in greeting.

'We could say the same thing about you, Little Miss Skiver!' retorted Luke as he came to stand on one side of her.

'Now now you two, play nice or I won't buy you an ice cream,' said Mr Harris, coming to stand on Maggie's other side. He took her hand and threaded her arm through his just as Luke draped his arm around her shoulders and pressed a kiss to her temple. Not wanting to be left out, McGregor plonked his behind down to sit on her feet.

McGregor, Harris, Harris and Henderson.

'My boys,' said Maggie, nodding at Stella in agreement. 'We'll be there.'

THE END

ALSO BY BETH RAIN

Seabury Series:

Welcome to Seabury (Seabury Book 1)

Trouble in Seabury (Seabury Book 2)

Christmas in Seabury (Seabury Book 3)

Sandwiches in Seabury (Seabury Book 4)

Secrets in Seabury (Seabury Book 5)

Surprises in Seabury (Seabury Book 6)

Dreams and Ice Creams in Seabury (Seabury Book 7)

Mistakes and Heartbreaks in Seabury (Seabury Book 8)

Laughter and Happy Ever After in Seabury (Seabury Book 9)

A Quiet Life in Seabury (Seabury Book 10)

In A Spin in Seabury (Seabury Book 11)

Living The Dream in Seabury (Seabury Book 12)

A Big Day in Seabury (Seabury Book 13)

Something Borrowed in Seabury (Seabury Book 14)

A Match Made in Seabury (Seabury Book 15)

Seabury Series Collections:

Kate's Story: Books 1 - 3

Hattie's Story: Books 4 - 6

Standalones: Books 7 - 9

Lizzie's Story: Books 10 - 12

Upper Bamton Series:

Upper Bamton: The Complete Series Collection: Books 1 - 4

Individual titles:

A New Arrival in Upper Bamton (Upper Bamton Book 1)

Rainy Days in Upper Bamton (Upper Bamton Book 2)

Hidden Treasures in Upper Bamton (Upper Bamton Book 3)

Time Flies By in Upper Bamton (Upper Bamton Book 4)

Standalone Books:

How to be Angry at Christmas

Crumbleton Series:

Coming Home to Crumbleton (Crumbleton Book 1)

Flowers Go Flying in Crumbleton (Crumbleton Book 2)

Match Point in Crumbleton (Crumbleton Book 3)

A Very Crumbleton Christmas (Crumbleton Book 4)

Little Bamton Series:

Little Bamton: The Complete Series Collection: Books 1 - 5

Individual titles:

Christmas Lights and Snowball Fights (Little Bamton Book 1)

Spring Flowers and April Showers (Little Bamton Book 2)

Summer Nights and Pillow Fights (Little Bamton Book 3)

Autumn Cuddles and Muddy Puddles (Little Bamton Book 4)

Christmas Flings and Wedding Rings (Little Bamton Book 5)

Crumcarey Island Series:

Crumcarey Island Series Collection: Books 1 - 5

Individual titles:

Christmas on Crumcarey (Crumcarey Island Book 1)

All Change on Crumcarey (Crumcarey Island Book 2)

Making Waves on Crumcarey (Crumcarey Island Book 3)

Fool's Gold on Crumcarey (Crumcarey Island Book 4)

A Fresh Start on Crumcarey (Crumcarey Island Book 5)

WRITING AS BEA FOX:

What's a Girl To Do? The Complete Series

Individual titles:

The Holiday: What's a Girl To Do? (Book 1)

The Wedding: What's a Girl To Do? (Book 2)

The Lookalike: What's a Girl To Do? (Book 3)

The Reunion: What's a Girl To Do? (Book 4)

At Christmas: What's a Girl To Do? (Book 5)

ABOUT THE AUTHOR

Beth Rain has always wanted to be a writer and has been penning adventures for characters ever since she learned to stare into the middle-distance and daydream.

She recently moved to a windswept, Scottish island, and it is a dream come true to spend her days hanging out with Bob – her trusty laptop – scoffing crisps and chocolate while dreaming up swoony love stories for all her imaginary friends.

Beth's writing will always deliver on the happy-ever-afters, so if you need cosy… you're in safe hands!

Visit www.bethrain.com for all the bookish goodness and keep up with all Beth's news by joining her monthly newsletter!

facebook.com/BethRainBooks
twitter.com/bethrainauthor
instagram.com/bethrainauthor

Printed in Great Britain
by Amazon